NEAAKA'S RAIN

A Journey through the Storms of Life

SYLVIA THOMPSON

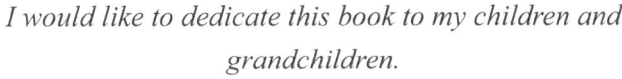

I would like to dedicate this book to my children and grandchildren.
It is just a brief glimpse of what it was like to grow up in the 1940s.

ISBN 978-0-9992755-8-0
Wiltshire Books LLC

Cover and interior design by https://www.jschlenker.com/

Photo: Eutha Scragg

Contents

Acknowledgments

I would like to thank my daughter Kathy for her boundless patience in helping me with the Word program. I would also like to thank the members of The Patchwork Writers Group for their constant encouragement.

Introduction

Neaaka's (knee-ock-ah) Rain is the story of a fourteen-year-old-girl who is beginning to feel the pain of growing up. She has been so sheltered and protected from the outside world that she is totally innocent of its pits and downfalls. Living in the head of a holler and working since the age of five she was just about convinced that's all there was to life until she started having feelings for a young man at church. He was five years older. She started writing him letters without her mother's knowledge. This led to a life of tragedy that she never could have imagined. By the time she is twenty-two she has experienced the deaths of two of her children and survived rape and murder, but also found true love. Her strength of character and her desire to succeed led her to another life.

This story is written as fiction, but the stories are based on truth.

Coming of Age

May 9, 1940

*D*ear Evan,

Momma says girls my age should not be writing to boys, but I think fourteen is old enough to know my own mind. Now whether or not it is proper is another question. Sometimes I think so hard and fast it gives me a headache. Papa says I talk so much I give him a headache too. I talk a lot to my family, but I'm very shy around other people. I saw you at church last Sunday, and I so hoped you would ask to walk me home. I don't want you to think I am too forward, but if a girl doesn't ask for what she wants, she may never get it. I learned that from my momma. She never asks for anything, so she never gets anything, not even a good word.

Grandpa says we are headed for a big war; he can feel

it in his bones. It's probably just arthritis. Every night he makes us sit around the radio and listen to the news. We are not allowed to speak when it is on because he might miss a word. Old people are so old-fashioned don't you think?

I will take a walk down to Nancy Jane's Grocery Store and mail this letter before I get admonished severely by my momma. I love going down to Nancy Jane's and looking at *The Saturday Evening Post* and learning new words. The pictures are nice too. I love learning new things.

Please feel free to walk me home anytime.

Yours Truly,
Neaaka Hollister

June 21, 1940

*D*ear Evan,

I'm sorry I didn't speak to you at the feed store on Monday. I'm really very shy, but when I have pen and paper in hand, oh how free I am. Maybe someday I'll be a famous writer like Mark Twain.

I saw you wink at me, and so did my papa. He asked me what that was all about and I told him nothing. That's the truth isn't it?

I kept looking for you when we stopped at the general store, but you never showed up.

Are you coming to the church social on Sunday after church? I hope so. Maybe we could do the cake walk together. I know you've never looked my way except to tease me, but I so hope someday you will. My papa says I shouldn't get my hopes up about finding a man because if there's a war like Grandpa thinks, they will all be going away. Papa and Grandpa are sure we are headed for a war. Don't you think old men are always looking for trouble?

If you come to the church social you can walk me home.

Yours Truly,

Neaaka

July 14, 1940

*D*ear Evan,

You weren't very friendly at the church social, and who was that girl you were with? I didn't think she was very pretty. I'm going to church Wednesday night. Maybe you would like to walk me home.

Grandpa keeps talking about going to war. You don't really think there's anything to that do you?

Sometimes I get so lonesome for somebody to talk to. My brothers are so much younger, and my sisters are a few years older. My oldest sister Alice thinks she's big stuff now that she's married and lives over in Kelsey. Vonetta will be getting married soon, and Kalinda is staying over in Kelsey with my Aunt Martha.

Momma says I talk so much I make people's ears tired. Do you think that's true Evan? Is it different if you're reading it? Do your eyes get tired from reading all that I write?

With Warmest Regards,
Neaaka

November 8, 1940

*D*ear Evan,

    Grandpa is at it again. He's carrying on about some guy named Hitler. He gets real upset when he talks about him. I don't see what that has to do with us, do you?

Papa is mad at me again. He told me to saddle Big Red and put his bridle on. Big Red did not want it on, so I told him it was okay and I rode him bareback down to Nancy Jane's Grocery Store. Next time I will put a saddle on him even if he doesn't want it, for my sake if not his. I had to hold onto his mane since I didn't put a bridle on. I had a dickens of a time trying to stay on him. I had to walk all the way back home carrying a twenty-five pound sack of flour. Guess I'll listen to Papa next time.

My sister Kalinda is still at Aunt Martha's. I guess she is going to try and meet someone and get married. Lord knows there's no one around here. When she came by for a visit last Sunday, she brought some silk underwear. I know I shouldn't talk to a man about such things, but I don't think it's the same if you're writing it, do you?

Anyway, I'd never seen silk underwear before: I just knew about muslin and feed sack underwear. I asked her if I could wear a pair just to see what it was like, and she said no real loud, even after I offered her a dime. I didn't have a dime, but I could have owed her. I thought that was just plain mean, don't you? Evan, a bunch of neighbors are getting together on Saturday to help Mr. Sansom build a new barn. I hope you will be there.

Momma is cooking and bringing some food over. I'll have to help with serving and watch after the little children. I sure would like to watch you too. Hope to see you there.

Yours truly,
Neaaka

November 18, 1940

*D*ear Evan,
I'm so glad you came to help with Mr. Sansom's barn. It was good to talk to you a few minutes before Papa gave you the evil eye. But he's harmless, I think.

When I was serving you lunch and you touched my hand, I had a funny feeling. What do you think that was? I asked my momma and she said, "Nice girls don't talk about that stuff." Evan, I'm confused. I don't know what stuff I'm not supposed to talk about.

Grandpa made us listen to the radio last night. There was something about Greece repelling the Italian invasion. Grandpa was all upset again. If he doesn't like what the radio has to say, why does he listen to it? There was also something about Hungary and Romania signing the Tripar-tite Pact and becoming part of the axis aligning itself with Germany, Italy and Japan. Grandpa was so upset he cursed. Papa just grinned and turned off the radio. Anyway, that's on the other side of the world, so what difference does it make.

My little brothers and I are going down to the general store on Saturday afternoon. Would you like to go? It could be fun. Thanks for helping Mr. Sansom.

Sincerely,
Neaaka

December 5, 1940

*D*ear Evan,

I'm so tired of staying in the house. It's too cold to go outside much except to do chores. Sometimes I just have to have a little fresh air.

Momma made some new curtains for my room today. It will be a nice change. Momma went to the feed store last summer with Papa to pick out the feed sacks she wanted to use to make my curtains.

I put on a big heavy coat and went outside tonight and laid on the swing for a while. I kept looking up into a sea of black sky. Evan, the sky is so big. It's like a big black ocean. Of course I've never seen an ocean, but I've seen pictures, and it looks soooo big. It sparkles like diamonds, not that I know what diamonds look like either, but I've heard that they sparkle. The stars are beautiful. I wonder what it would be like to go to the stars and visit. Maybe I'll stop by and visit on my way to heaven. I don't think it ever hurts to use your imagination, do you?

Grandpa has been listening to that radio all month long. He just fusses and carries on every day. Sometimes I wish he would just wear that battery out. He said the United States began the first peacetime draft. I guess that means something to him, but not to me. He just went on and on about President Roosevelt asking Joe Kennedy, whoever that is, to resign as ambassador to the United Kingdom. He said he gave a newspaper interview and said that democracy is finished in England.

Evan, I don't mean to sound mean. I think I just need a little sunshine to lift my spirits. It will be Christmas in a few days. I guess Papa will be going to the City Market in Memphis to buy some fruit and candy for Christmas. I'm sure that will cheer me up.

I went over to close those curtains Momma made for me. It was just weird how those little ol' curtains held back that big night sky.

Evan, it sure would be nice if you would write to me. I love getting mail. Guess I will close for now.

Yours Truly,
Neaaka

A Different Life

1941

January 16, 1941

*D*ear Evan,

It was so nice to see you on Christmas Day at church. Momma would be mad if she knew I was writing to you. She thinks it is very unlady like.

Christmas was really nice. Papa went to the City Market in Memphis and bought lots of candy and fruit. We could eat all we wanted, and that was Christmas. I've heard that there are people who buy presents for each other, but I've never seen anyone do that. It's a good thing Christmas comes only once a year. I thought I was going to turn into a banana.

Momma hasn't been feeling well. I think she may have

dropsy, because every time she sees a chair she drops into it. Maybe she just has the winter blues. I've been feeling sort of blue too. I guess it must be the weather, it being so cold and all. It's too bad it doesn't snow much here in Mason; if it did, maybe I wouldn't feel so blue.

Grandpa heard on the radio that Charles Lindbergh testified before the U.S. Congress and recommended that the United States negotiate a neutrality pact with Adolf Hitler. What do you think that means? Grandpa is so determined that we are going to war. I don't know why he keeps saying that; he's too old to fight anyway. He must be fifty years old.

My little brother Luke fell in the creek Sunday on the way home from church. I laughed, and Papa kicked me on the behind but not very hard. The worst part was getting his muddy footprint off my coat. Daddy took his coat off and wrapped it around Luke. He looked like a little icicle by the time we walked the rest of the way home.

I had to go out Wednesday and chop some wood. Papa took Big Red back on the hill and hauled a couple of big logs down. He and I took the cross-cut saw and cut them up. I had to take the wedge and split the wood. I got really tired. Papa said you rest only when the job is finished and not until.

Evan, someday I'm going to have a maid, and I'll make her chop all the wood and wash all the dishes, then I'll get dropsy like my momma and sit in a chair all day.

Evan, are you looking forward to spring? I sure am. In

a couple of weeks Momma is going to let me go visit my aunts, Aunt Mabel and Aunt Martha. Mabel lives in a little town called Sweet Run which is just on the other side of Kelsey. My Aunt Martha actually lives in Kelsey. Aunt Mabel is going to teach me how to sew. I'll take some feed sacks and turn them into some beautiful things. Just wait and see. Maybe I'll wear something I made to church.

I'll write again next month. I'd write more often, but Momma would notice that her stamps and stationery are missing. This way she doesn't notice, but if she did I'd have to tell her the truth because I don't want to go to hell for lying.

Evan, why don't you ever write back to me? It would be so wonderful to get a letter in the mail. I walk down to the mailbox every day to pick up the mail, but there's never anything for me. The mail is always for Papa and sometimes Grandpa. Hope to see you at church on Sunday.

Best Regards,
Neaaka

February 16, 1941

*D*ear Evan,

Christmas is over, and I'm trying real hard to feel and smell spring in the air, so far no luck. Don't you get excited when the little green leaves start to sprout. It's like a resurrection. First it was dead, and then it is reborn.

I went over to Aunt Mabel's, and she gave me a few sewing lessons. I must say it's going to take a lot of practice. I made a circle-tail skirt, and the back was about six inches shorter than the front. Aunt Mabel was frustrated because I wasted the feed sack material. We added another ruffle and made it a little wider in the back than in the front. It will be okay to feed the chickens and slop the hogs, but you'll never see me in it.

I met a girl over at Aunt Mabel's. She is her neighbor. She is a year older than me and very pretty. I think I'll write to her also. Her name is Loretta Wiley. She has a boyfriend, but I don't think she likes him very much.

Momma said I should start making aprons, and then if I make a mistake it wouldn't be so noticeable. I'm kind of worried about Momma. I teased her about having dropsy, and she just laughed. I believe something may be wrong. She doesn't have a lot of energy and asks me to do a lot more. Of course I don't mind, but it isn't like her. I asked her to go see Dr. Green. She says it costs too much and that she is just tired but expects to be fine in a few days.

When Grandpa turns on the radio, I try to disappear now. I heard him and Papa talking about some guy named Admiral Husband Kimmel. What kind of name is that? They said he was appointed the Commander of the U. S. Navy in the Pacific, and Lieutenant General Erwin Rommel was appointed the head of something called the Germany Army Troops in Africa. Grandpa says they are building up troops and getting ready for something big. Grandpa has been reading his Bible a lot more lately. Wonder what that means?

Aunt Mabel gave my little brother Luke a bazooka gun. It shoots little white balls. It only had three balls with it, and he had lost two of them, but I didn't know that. The little gun was lying in the side yard, and I picked it up and shot it. The ball went into the pig pen, and the old sow ate it for dinner. Luke came out of the house with an ice pick and chased me around the house. He stabbed me in the side a little bit; it made a small red place. Momma was going to give him what for. I begged her not to because it was my fault. I guess I'll have to save the egg money and buy him some new white balls. It seems like the right thing to do.

Evan, I heard that you were dating Anna Mae Lovett. If that is true, and you want me to stop writing to you, I will. I just hope it's all a big fat lie and not a skinny little truth.

Well, I guess I'd better close and save some chatter for next time.

Til next time,
Neaaka

May 16, 1941

*D*ear Evan,
I missed writing you in March and April. Momma has been really sick. Papa finally took her to see Dr. Green. He gave her some green medicine. He said it would calm her nerves. She's in a lot of pain. I don't know a whole lot about medicine, but I thought nerves made you jittery and don't cause a lot of pain.

I don't have much time any more. I have to do my chores plus Momma's. Those two little boys are a handful. Last Wednesday I just needed some peace and quiet, so I gave Levi five pennies and told him to go out by the fence and plant them so he could grow a money tree. It kept him busy for about ten minutes. Finally he and Luke went down by the creek to play.

I'm really worried about Momma. Some days she doesn't get up at all, and she hardly eats anything. I guess I can understand that. I'm just learning to cook. Maybe I wouldn't eat it either.

Momma said that I became a woman this past winter, I guess that's a good thing because I sure was tired of being a little girl. Of course some of the things a woman has to go through are no fun either.

I'll be fifteen in a few days. Sometimes I feel older than my years, and sometimes I feel like a little kid. Life sure can be confusing.

Papa and Grandpa burned a tobacco bed in March and sowed some tobacco seeds. They burned a lettuce bed also. We've already had lettuce and onions from the garden. They've also plowed the garden and one cornfield. The tobacco fields have been plowed as well. They will be setting out the tobacco plants any day now. We will all have a lot to do this summer. I will be teaching Luke to hoe the garden. He's five now, and that's plenty old enough. Last summer I tried to teach him to hoe the tomatoes. After I went back into the house, he decided to help and cut down all the tomato plants. Papa had a conniption fit.

Levi is old enough to bring water to us when we need it. Everyone has a job to do. I'm glad I'm being taught to work. The girl I met over in Sweet Run doesn't know how to do much of anything. Her mother does everything for her. I think that's pretty sad.

Levi goes out every day to see if his money tree is growing. I don't have the heart to tell him it's not going to happen.

Well, I will close for now. I'm sure it would be all right if you would stop by sometime or write me a letter.

Yours Truly,
Neaaka

June 4, 1941

*D*ear Neaaka,
I'm so sorry to hear about your mother's passing. She was a lovely lady. Clarence Perkins stopped by today and told us about it. He's waiting downstairs to bring this note to you.

Neaaka, I know I haven't paid much attention to you, but when you didn't write in March or April, I missed your letters. I thought about stopping by but just couldn't get up the nerve. I feel like I've gotten to know you from your letters. You sound like a sweet girl, but you are very young. I'm sure someday you will make some man a very fine wife.

I know you have a lot of responsibility now helping to raise your little brothers. Maybe I could help your papa and grandpa if they need help bringing in the crops this fall. Please tell them I will be glad to help if I'm still here. You know President Roosevelt enacted a peacetime draft, and I'm the right age. I may go ahead and enlist. I'll have to think about it for a while.

I will be at your mother's wake, we'll talk then.

I've got to get this downstairs so Clarence can bring this note to you. I'm sure my mom will bring food or send food for the wake. Again, just know how sorry I am for your loss.

My Deepest Sympathy,
Evan

June 20, 1941

*D*ear Neaaka,

My, how you've changed over the winter. You don't look like the little girl I remember from church last summer. I know you've been through a tough time, and sometimes that makes a person grow up fast, but you grew out in other places also. I was pleasantly surprised.

I enjoyed our conversation at your Mother's wake. I know it's very sad for you to have her home one more time to say goodbye. You were very brave.

Neaaka, would it be okay for me to stop by sometime just to talk? I really enjoyed our time together. Make sure it's okay with your Papa. Tell him if he needs any work done I would be glad to help.

When you first started writing me, I was annoyed when your letters came, and then I started looking forward to them. I think we've got a lot in common. I'd like the chance to get to know you better.

Until I see you again,
Evan

July 7, 1941

*D*ear Loretta,

It was so nice of you to come to Momma's wake with Aunt Mabel. I think we could be very good friends. What did you think of Evan? He has been so nice through all of this.

I tried to make Luke a shirt this week, but one side was longer than the other, so I cut it off, and now it's too short, and the other side is long. Papa will be real mad if I waste the material. I just don't know how else to learn. I can't go back to Aunt Mabel's for more sewing lessons. I have to be here with the boys.

We went to church Sunday, and that ol' Ellie Parsons was making eyes at my papa. My momma hasn't been gone two months yet. I was so mad on the way home. Papa asked me what was wrong, and I told him. He laughed. He thought it was funny, but I don't. I don't want some other old woman coming in here and trying to tell me what to do.

Loretta, life is much harder now than it was when Momma was here. Sometimes I cry myself to sleep. I told Grandpa it wasn't fair that Momma left us. He said, "Sis, I'm going to tell you something, and you'd better remember it. Life isn't fair, it just isn't. The Lord gives us trials and temptations, and how we handle them is how we please the Lord. That's what it's all about; it's how you do the Lord's work. No, it's not fair, that's just the way it is! Get used to it."

If Grandpa was trying to comfort me, he failed miserably.

I never knew a woman's work on the farm could be so hard. I taught Levi how to feed the chickens and gather the eggs. The first day he threw half of them away because they had chicken poop on them. I had to explain they were to be washed. He said he wasn't eating anything with chicken poop on it. I'm pretty sure I don't want kids.

Loretta, Aunt Mabel said she would come by from time to time and check on us. I hope you will come with her. After Momma died, my sisters just left and went back to their own lives. They said I was a big girl, and I could handle things. I don't want to be a big girl. I just want things to go back to the way they were when Momma was here.

I'm sorry I'm being such a whiny girl. Why would you want to be my friend? I will try and liven up when I write you again. Thanks for listening.

Best Regards,
Neaaka

November 10, 1941

ear Evan,

It was so good to see you on Sunday.

That ol' Ellie Parsons came over on Sunday after church and brought a big platter of fried chicken. I just know she's trying to get her hooks into my papa. She looks like she's been hit in the face with a shovel and has prunes for lips. That sounds really bad, doesn't it?

While she was here, she was complaining about Luke and Levi's manners. I told her their manners are fine, you don't have to worry about them. She looked at Papa and said, "Well, she's an insolent little thing isn't she?"

Papa said, "Neaaka, mind your manners."

I think I saw red. Of course I would never talk back to Papa.

Evan, I know Papa will probably get married again someday, but it doesn't have to be to the likes of her. She's got a boy in the army. She started talking about the war in Europe. Truth be told, she should marry Grandpa. He's always talking about a war. They could just fight it out.

Evan, I've got a whole lot of mad built up in me. I'm not going to let that ol' Ellie Parsons ruin our family. Do you know any nice pretty women we could fix my papa up with? That would put a dent in her old bucket face.

Papa told me my attitude wasn't very Christian-like,

and I know that's true. I'm still not going to let her ruin our family.

Evan, I hope you can come by next week. We have to work out a plan.

Yours in cahoots,

Neaaka

November 14, 1941

*D*ear Neaaka,

I am so happy to have a new friend to share things with. I love writing letters and getting them in the mail. It gives me something to look forward to. I'm glad you feel like you can tell me things. I will not repeat anything you tell me not to. I think it's very important to be a loyal friend.

Evan seemed real nice. He sure was paying a lot of attention to you. Your grandpa was watching very closely.

I know it will be very hard with your mother gone, but my momma says you will learn a lot very quickly about being able to take care of the boys and chores around the house. Personally, I think you are a little young to be dealing with all that.

I know you will learn to sew and get it right fairly soon. I was wondering if your Aunt Mabel could teach me to sew.

Neaaka, I let my boyfriend kiss me two nights ago. I didn't think I liked him very much, but his kiss really felt good. I wanted him to do it again. He didn't offer, so I let it go. When he first put his arms around me, I felt all warm and fuzzy inside. Has Evan ever kissed you? I hope you will tell me if he does. We girls have to behave properly, but sometimes it's very hard. We just have to be careful some old busy body isn't watching everything we do.

Will close for now.
Write soon.
Loretta

November 22, 1941

*D*ear Loretta,

I'm so upset. What I'm about to tell you, you must promise to never, never tell a single soul for the rest of your life. I can't believe it happened. I am so heartsick. I've got to get out of here and find another place to live, but I'm only fifteen. I don't know what to do.

Two days ago I was changing the mantle in the gas light in the front room. I climbed upon a chair. Grandpa came through and told me to be careful and not touch the mantle itself, or I would ruin it, like I didn't know that already. Then Papa came in, but I didn't hear him. When I turned around, he was just staring at me. I've never been uncomfortable around my papa, but I had an uneasy feeling. I said, "Hi, Papa" and he nodded in my direction.

I stepped down off the chair and headed out to the kitchen. Papa grabbed me by the forearms and pinned me against the wall. Loretta, he pressed himself against me until I could feel his private parts. I was so disgusted all I could do was cry. When he saw the tears, he let me go and said, "My God, what am I doing?" He ran out of the house and down to the barn.

Loretta, I don't know what any of it means, but I don't like it here anymore. I can't just up and leave. I have no place to go. Luke and Levi have to have someone to take care of them. I just feel dirty, and I don't know why. I haven't done anything. I feel like you are the only one I can talk to. I trust you not to say anything to anyone, please, please, not even to Aunt Mabel. I wish she would come and stay with us for a while.

Grandpa is still convinced there's going to be a war. If I was a boy, I sure would join up. My insides feel sick whenever Papa walks into the room. He doesn't look at me anymore, and he doesn't talk to me. He tells the boys to tell me what to do. Loretta, what does it mean when a man does that to a girl? I just don't understand. Momma told me when I became a woman that I could have a baby, so I shouldn't let boys touch me. Charlie Cameron put his hand on my back coming down the church steps, but I didn't have a baby, now this. Do you think I will have a baby now? I just don't understand what it all means.

Loretta, I really want to tell Evan, but for some reason I'm afraid. I feel like this is private. This is why I'm telling you. I thought I was going to explode inside if I didn't tell someone.

I will write Aunt Mabel and ask her to come. I will never ever mention this to another living soul. Loretta, please destroy this letter after you read it. No other eyes should ever look upon it. How I long for my carefree days as a child when Momma was here to take care of me and my brothers and sisters. I will never breathe a word of this to my sisters. They would think I am lying, and I'm not. Loretta, if you have any words of wisdom I could use them about now. Papa brought me a fancy piece of material home the other day. He handed it to me and never said a word. He did look me in the eye though. It's been a while since he's done that. I don't know what he wants me to do with it. Guess I'll have to ask him. Things just aren't the same since Momma passed on.

I went to the feed store yesterday and saw that ol' Ellie Parsons. I didn't speak to her at first, but after I walked by, I heard her tell Mr. Dawson that I was a half-breed. "Why she's got more Indian in her than her mother had," she said. "Now those little boys don't seem to have as much. I'll never understand what Sam Hollister saw in that bunch of half-breeds. Now Sam, himself, is mighty pleasing to look at."

I just thought to myself, "Ol' lady you can have Sam Hollister and let him pin you up against the wall." Now I'm not one to hit people, but I wanted to grab a rake off the rack and rearrange her face. I got what I went for and headed home. All the way home I felt anger boiling up inside. I'm afraid it's going to spill over.

Loretta, this letter is getting long. I can't seem to stop. I want to leave and never come back, but my little brothers need me. I feel trapped. What am I going to do? I can't live here, and I can't go anywhere. Loretta, please write soon. I have no one to talk to about anything.

Yours truly,
Neaaka

November 30, 1941

*D*ear Neaaka,

I am in shock. When I read your letter I gasped. My momma asked me what was wrong. I made up a story to tell her. I felt really bad about it, but I don't have a lot of friends, and I did not want to let you down. I don't know how you are coping. Your papa seems like such a nice man. I guess we never know what evil lurks beneath. I got that from the radio show "The Shadow."

I talked to your Aunt Martha Saturday. Don't worry I didn't tell her anything. She said she and your Aunt Mabel were thinking of coming over and staying a few days.

My momma sometimes looks through the *National Bella Hess* catalog and finds a pretty dress she wants to make. She will take a dress she already has and add extra things to it just like in the picture. Momma could never teach me to sew. She says she doesn't have the patience. That's why I hoped your Aunt Mabel could teach me.

Neaaka, I'm at a loss for words about what happened to you. Maybe I could come and stay with you a while when school is out. You will be fifteen in May; maybe things will be better then. I will never ever tell another single living soul. You can count on me.

I will try and write more often. I can't imagine being up that holler and never seeing anyone except your papa and grandpa and little brothers. Looks like your sisters would give you some support. I guess they're just tickled to be out of there.

There are several young men in town who are talking about not waiting on the draft but joining up right away. It will be very strange not having any young men around. What if they all get killed, Neaaka? We will be old maids and never get married or have children. That would be so sad. Do you think Evan will go ahead and sign up for the army? You could still write to him.

Will close for now. Write soon and let me know what's going on.

Yours Truly,
Loretta

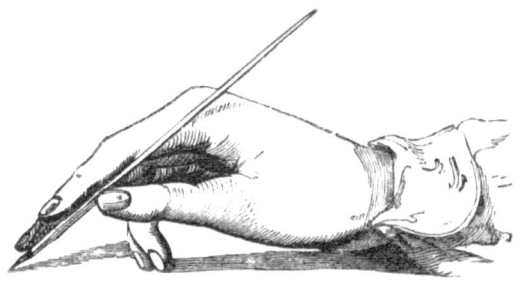

November 30, 1941

*D*ear Neaaka,

Hope this letter finds you well and happy. The last letter I received from you was a little disturbing. I got the feeling that something was wrong, but I don't know what. You know you can tell me anything.

I went over to the county courthouse today and inquired about signing up for the army. I'm a little older than most guys going in because I got a delay since I was sole support for my mom and dad when Dad was so sick. Things are a little better now than they were. Everyone's excited about doing their part for the war. War hasn't been declared yet, but they need people to get ready just in case. Personally, I think it's a little scary.

I'll be over Friday night. I've got something I want to talk to you about. I've really enjoyed our conversations. You're a wonderful girl. I'm so sorry it took me so long to figure that out. I hope your papa is there also. I want to talk to him.

You really do have your hands full there, don't you? My mom has been sad all day, ever since she found out I went to the courthouse. She told me about her father going off to the First World War. I'd heard about that before, but it really didn't mean anything to me until today. Sometimes men have to do what they think is right regardless of what other people think.

When you met my mother at your momma's wake, what did you think of her?

She's a really good person. You'd like her if you could spend more time with her, and I'm sure she'd like you.

Neaaka, I will close for now and will see you Friday night.

Yours Truly,

Evan

December 10, 1941

*D*ear Evan,

It looks like Grandpa was right. Aunt Mabel got Mr. Crosby, one of her neighbors, to bring her over today. She had a copy of the *Tennessee Herald* newspaper. She and Grandpa were so excited they could hardly talk. Papa did not seem too interested one way or the other. I didn't think Grandpa was ever going to let me see the newspaper, but he finally laid it down after he read the whole thing. He kept saying, "I was right. I knew it was going to happen."

The headlines, I think that's what they are called, said in great big letters **Jap Planes, Ships Waging War on the U.S.** The newspaper says two Japanese bombers bearing the insignia of the rising sun appeared over Honolulu about 7:35 a.m. today and dropped bombs. I think Honolulu is in New England somewhere. I hope it's not close to us. The army and navy have sprung into action.

What does that mean, Evan? It says untold damage has been done to the U.S. Naval Base at Pearl Harbor and to the city of Honolulu. Lots of unmarked planes were unidentified. I guess that means they didn't have the rising sun on them. Grandpa says all the young men around here will be joining the service.

I don't like being almost grown up. It's so complicated. I hate living here now. Papa doesn't speak to me anymore. I'm so miserable, Evan, and there's not a thing I can do about it. If it weren't for the boys, I would go live with one of my sisters or Aunt Mabel. I have no one to talk to except for the little boys. I love them dearly, but I need something else. I write to my friend Loretta sometimes. You met her here when Momma died. It's only been a few months, but it seems like a lifetime ago. I don't mean to complain, so I'll stop.

It's starting to get real cold. Momma would be gathering up quilt pieces and getting ready to make a beautiful quilt. Maybe I will too. Evan, if you go off to service will you come and say goodbye to me first? I hope I can still write to you if you go away.

Papa brought me a fancy piece of material home the other day. He handed it to me and never said a word. He did look me in the eye though. It's been awhile since he's done that. I don't know what he wants me to do with it. Things just aren't the same since Momma passed on.

Evan, do you have any idea what this war on the U.S. means? I have a really bad feeling about all this. Mr. Dawson from the feed store came all the way out here today and talked to Papa and Grandpa about Pearl Harbor. His son Caleb is about to turn eighteen, so I guess he will be going to war too. That could explain why he looked so troubled.

Evan, I've got to go now, it's time to get stuff from the cellar for supper.

Neaaka

December 12, 1941

*D*ear Loretta,

Evan was here every night last week. He and Papa talked a lot. So did we.

Loretta, he kissed me. My knees felt like Momma's jelly, and my toes tingled. What do you think that means? I really liked it. It scared me though. Feelings are such weird things, don't you think? I wonder what love feels like. Do you suppose that could have been it? I wish Momma were here so I could talk to her. I can't ask Papa, 'cause he doesn't understand anything.

Aunt Martha and Aunt Mabel are coming over next week. I got a letter from Aunt Mabel today. I do so love getting letters in the mail. I guess next week is as good a time as any for my aunts to visit. It's too cold to go out much anyway. Evan asked me a lot of strange questions. He asked me if I'd ever thought about getting out of this holler. I told him, "All the time." There's no way I could leave my little brothers though. He said maybe I could take them with me. Papa would never stand for that.

Evan held me in his arms for a long time and said he wanted to make things better for me. I don't know how he could make things better if he's leaving for the army. He's coming over after church on Sunday. Guess I'll have to kill a chicken on Saturday and put it in brine for Sunday dinner. Grandpa says I have turned into a pretty good cook.

Papa still doesn't talk to me and will not stay in the same room as me. It makes me feel guilty like I did something wrong. Even Luke and Levi are beginning to ask what's wrong. I just tell them Papa's having a hard time with Momma being gone, and that's the truth up to a certain point.

Grandpa listens to the radio a lot now to keep up with the war. Grandpa wants to keep up with what he calls "the devastation of Pearl Harbor." He's wishing he was a young man so he could go fight. The radio doesn't bother me like it used to. I guess I've grown up a little bit.

The last two shirts I made for the boys turned out okay. I heard Papa telling the boys they looked real good, but he didn't tell me I did a good job. Being almost grown up is so hard. Grandpa says, "What don't kill us will make us stronger." I hope that's true.

I feel like I really need to talk to Papa about what happened. I'm afraid if we let it go and go, it will be like a big ol' blackhead and fester until it just bursts. I'm afraid we may never be able to talk about it if we don't talk now. That would be so sad. I used to love my papa and really want to again. If I could just understand, maybe things would be all right. I think I'll start speaking to him again when he's in the room. Maybe that will help.

Loretta, sometimes I feel like I'm running backwards through a henhouse trying not to step on the eggs. Life's hard.

I will write you next week and tell you about Evan's visit.

Til next time,
Neaaka

December 14, 1941

*D*ear Loretta,

Well, Sunday came and went, and I am so confused. I liked it better when my biggest concern was getting chicken poop off my feet when I gathered eggs.

Evan asked me to marry him. He asked me if I wanted to go for a walk. I really didn't because it was so cold. I told him that, but he didn't seem to care, he just wanted me to go outside with him. We walked up to the well, and he stopped. He put his arms around me, and I thought my knees were going to buckle. He said he'd been thinking about me a lot lately. He talked about going off to war and what a good woman his mother was. Then he asked me to marry him. I think I really want to. Evan thinks I should stay with his mother while he's gone. I don't know her.

I've seen her at church and at my momma's wake. She didn't look like a happy person. I talked to Evan about the boys. He said maybe I could keep them sometimes at his mama's house.

Loretta, I talked to Papa Monday. I asked him why he did what he did. He cried and said he was weak in his faith, and the devil got hold of him. He said he was so sorry, and he would rather lay down his life than hurt me. He said Evan had talked to him about us getting married. He thinks I should wait another year.

Papa has been seeing that ol' Ellie Parsons. He said she would help with the boys.

Evan is going to enlist in January. He wanted to wait until after Christmas. I told him I would let him know by this coming Sunday. There sure is a heap of stuff going through my head right now.

Aunt Martha and Aunt Mabel are coming over this coming week to help me sew up that material Papa got for me. Maybe we will make a wedding dress. Imagine me in a wedding dress. I don't know what to do. I know I'm rambling all over the place. I want to be excited, but I'm too scared. I feel like I'm standing on the sharp jagged edges of change and about to fall into an abyss. I learned that word from reading *Life Magazine* down at Nancy Jane's Grocery Store.

Loretta, what does it mean to be married? Do they just sleep in the same bed, and the woman does all the house and garden work? Are we just free labor? I sure wish Momma were here to talk to. I don't know why I just couldn't stay with Papa after we get married and help out with the boys. Papa said it was up to me. He would understand if I wanted to leave and not blame me.

When you get married, do you have to do everything your husband says? If that is true, I can tell you right now I'm going to have a problem with it. I wish there were more boys around so maybe I could have a choice. If I don't marry Evan right now, I may be an old maid and never have children. I'm fifteen already.

Momma always said, "When your burdens are too heavy, just pray and ask the Lord to help you carry the load." She said it always works. So I guess we will be having a talk later today, because my load sure is heavy.

Grandpa says that this Hitler guy has just taken over the Post of Commander in Chief of the German Army.

Christmas is only three days away. I'm baking today. There's always lots of food for Christmas. I made the boys shirts and crocheted mittens and scarves for both boys.

Loretta, I will write next Monday and tell you about my dress Hopefully, we will get it finished this week. I'm still in a quandary about what to do, but you can see which way I'm leaning.

Thanks for being there,
Neaaka

Innocence Gone

1942

January 14, 1942

*D*ear Vonetta,

I enjoyed your visit last week. I've missed you since you got married and moved over to Sweet Run. I really wanted to talk to you but never got the chance. I'm not sure what it means to be married, and so far I can't find anyone to tell me what to expect. I thought maybe my big sister could fill me in. I'm so scared.

Have you heard from Alice? I think I'll write to her soon. She's only been home twice since she moved out.

I think I really love Evan. But to stay with his mother while he's gone to the army scares me more than marrying him.

Evan took me over to visit his parents last Sunday. His mother is so proper. I was a nervous wreck. I dropped a piece of potato in my lap while we were eating. I looked around real quick to see if anyone was looking, no one was, so I just left it there until we were finished eating. His mother's name is Doris, and his father's name is Cleveland. Everyone just calls him Cleve. He's very nice.

Doris has lots of books, why there must be at least twenty. I found a book of poetry by Emily Dickinson. Once I started reading it, I just couldn't put it down. The words were like music on paper. She let me borrow it. I have read it all the way through and have started it again. I don't understand it all, but I enjoy learning so much. The words were so beautiful. Who knew you could put words together like that? It's kind of like designing a dress, you put all the pieces together, and they fit. I'm so excited about the poetry and getting married. Sometimes I think God has me mixed up with somebody else and is giving me all their blessings. Lord knows I don't deserve all that's going on right now.

Evan is leaving on January 27, and we are getting married on the 20th. We will only have one week before he leaves.

I told Luke and Levi that I would be moving over to Evan's house, and they cried like their little hearts were broken.

They followed me around the house and begged and begged me not to go. My heart broke also. They are so scared. I'll have to make sure I get back to see them often. It's only fifteen miles or so. I could walk or borrow one of Cleve's horses. Luke said he would be good and not put a frog in my shoe anymore. Levi said he would quit having bad dreams and waking me up. I already miss them. Papa says they will be fine. That ol' Ellie Parsons will make herself indispensable until Papa thinks he can't get along without her.

Vonnie, if you have any advice for me, now would be the time. I told Nancy Jane at the grocery store that I was getting married, and she looked at me real funny, like she knew something that I didn't. I was embarrassed that I told her. Something just did not feel right. Wonder what that was about?

I asked Aunt Martha to tell me about getting married. She said as long as I take care of my wifely duties every-thing should be fine. She said some women didn't mind their duties, and some did, but she said, "If you don't like them you should never let your husband know."

I told her it was too late I had already told Evan that I like to do house cleaning and farm chores. Aunt Martha covered her mouth with her hand and snickered, then tried to straighten her face up. I heard her telling Aunt Mabel, and they both snickered. I don't understand what it's all about.

Did you like my dress? Aunt Martha didn't want me to put the trim on it like that, but I wanted it to be just mine. It's the one I'm wearing to get married in. Papa said I could take Momma's sewing machine over to the Moores and maybe make some extra money with my sewing. I'm getting pretty good at it now, don't you think?

I'm going to write Kalinda also. Maybe she will have some advice for me, but seeing as she isn't married yet, maybe she won't.

Please write soon,
Neaaka

January, 19, 1942

*D*ear Neaaka,

I just loved your dress. You did a great job on it. The extra things you added were very elegant. It's a perfect wedding dress. It's a shame it will only be worn once, or maybe it could be passed along. I'm sure Kalinda will get married someday.

Neaaka, you asked me for some advice. I really don't know what to tell you, but I will say always put God first, and everything else will take care of itself. Do you remember Momma always saying that? Marriage is hard, but there are good things too. You always have someone to share things with. Your wifely duties can be as pleasant as you want to make them. They are very important to your husband. He gets all bent out of shape when they don't go well.

When you go to live at the Moores we'll be able to see each other more often since they live here in Sweet Run also. Kalinda is coming over to go to your wedding with me. I understand it will only be a few people. The Moores have a lovely home as you know. It will be a different life.

I may bring the boys over for a few weeks this summer. We can take them swimming and have a few picnics. The main thing is to see that they get a good education. They are both so smart, just like you. There are several young girls in Sweet Run. Maybe you could make their wedding dresses someday.

Neaaka, I just found out I am expecting a baby. I am so excited. The baby will be due the end of July or the first part of August. When we talk again in private, I will tell you a little more about your wifely duties. I'll see you next week at your wedding.

Your loving sister,
Vonetta

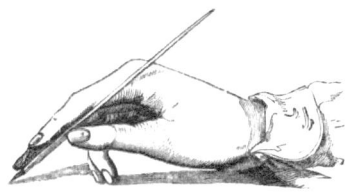

January 18, 1942

*D*ear Loretta,

This will be my last letter as a single girl. I guess I should call myself a woman since I'm getting married in a couple of days. There is so much to think about. I'm thinking about just closing my eyes and letting things happen. Then I will open them when everything is over. Everybody is making such a big fuss about getting married. Why do you think that is? I'm just moving from one house to another. I know people who have moved before. What's the big deal?

Papa is taking me over to Evan's Sunday after church, and the preacher is coming to dinner. Around five o'clock we will be getting married. It all seems so strange especially since Evan is leaving for the army. His mother isn't happy that he's going, but at the same time she's proud of him. I hope someday Papa will be proud of me.

I told Evan I would write to him every day. He said the recruiter told him about V-mail. That is where you write only on one side of the paper, and it is sent to Washington, D.C., where it is read by a censor, and they black out anything that might help the enemy if it falls into the wrong hands. It is then photographed and put on film. They can get 18,000 letters on one reel of film. When it arrives at its destination, it is printed on 3½-x-4-inch cards and given to the soldiers. He said there is so much mail that it takes up a lot of space on the cargo planes, and this way it takes up very little. Don't you think that's interesting? I guess as long as I let Evan know that he's not going to be the boss of me, that's all he needs to know. I'll be a good wife and write nice letters. Evan says letters are very important to the war effort. That is supposed to keep the morale up.

The next time I write to you I will be Mrs. Evan Moore. Don't you think it's strange that a woman takes on the man's name? Why couldn't he take on hers, or why couldn't they just keep their own names? There is so much to learn. While Evan is gone I'm going to read every one of Mrs. Moore's books.

I may not write any letters next week. I will probably wait until Evan has left, and that will give me something to do. Without Papa, Grandpa, and the boys filling up every minute of every day, I won't know what to do with myself. Of course, I'll help Mrs. Moore with chores and around the house, but it's so clean it won't take very long. I found out that she has a cleaning lady that comes in every two weeks and does the heavy stuff.

If you can, please come to my wedding with Aunt Martha. I want you to see my dress. It is the first thing I've ever made for myself that I will wear out in public. If Aunt Martha and Aunt Mabel had not helped me, I probably would have had to get married in a feed sack.

Loretta, I am so excited and scared. I just wish the next few days were over.

I asked Grandpa for some advice on getting married. He just looked at me and made a noise with his mouth and said, "Girl you'll learn." Then he looked like he felt sorry for me and turned and walked away. Things sure are confusing. I'll write you in a week or so. Thanks for being my friend.

Sincerely,

Neaaka

January 21, 1942

*D*ear Ms. Diary,

I am so angry. How stupid could I be? Why did no one tell me what wifely duties were? Why didn't Vonnie tell me? Oh God, Diary. Let me tell you what happened. Evan and I got married on Sunday. It was a great day with family and friends. When everyone left and the dishes were done, Mr. and Mrs. Moore excused themselves and went to bed. Evan and I sat in the parlor for a while. He had his arm around me, and it felt so right. I remembered when I first started writing to him how I dreamed about his arms being around me and now they were. Finally, he said we should go to bed. I felt really strange. I didn't feel comfortable about sleeping in the same bed as him, but I figured I would get used to it. My momma and papa slept in the same bed, and so do Mr. and Mrs. Moore, and I will too.

I made Evan turn his head while I put my nightgown on. Then I knelt by the bed to pray. Evan wasn't sure what to do, so I asked him to kneel with me. I figured he may as well get used to it. It was going to happen every night from now on. He didn't really seem to have much interest though. Then I got into bed. He got into bed and put his arms around me. It was then that I noticed he didn't have any clothes on. I held my breath. I was afraid to move. What had I gotten myself into? It was about this time that he slipped his hand under my gown. I jumped, and with one move I kicked him out of bed. He fell in the floor with such a thud that it woke his father. Mr. Moore hollered upstairs and said, "Evan, don't you hurt that girl."

Evan stood up and was holding his back. Oh my goodness, I had never seen a naked man before. Oh God, oh God, I'm praying, but I don't know for what. I thought I may not make it through the night.

Evan got back in bed and said, "What in the hell do you think you're doing?"

I snapped, "What do you think you're doing putting your hands on my body?"

He told me I'm his wife, and I will do as he says.

I looked him right in the eye and said, "Boy, do you have a lot to learn."

Evan lay there quietly for a while and then started laughing. By this time I'm really mad and have my back turned to him. He put his arm across me, and when I started to move, he told me just to be still, and we would talk. At least I didn't kick him this time. He explained about the birds and bees. He said that women didn't really mind their wifely duties once they got used to them. I asked him how many wives he had that he knew so much. He finally said we would say goodnight and talk tomorrow, which suited me just fine.

Early the next morning I awoke to Evan gently caressing my face and looking at me. He told me how pretty I was and how he loved me. He'd never said that before. He kissed me so tenderly that when it was time, I did my duty without complaint. He told me to get dressed, and we would go down to breakfast. It was then I realized that his mama and papa knew what we had been doing. How would I ever be able to face them? Everyone who sees me is going to know that I had done things that I'd only seen animals do. Oh God, I prayed, I'm going to have to spend the rest of my life in this room. I am never going out where people could see me. When I didn't go down to breakfast, Evan came looking for me. When I told him I had to stay in our room because I couldn't face his parents, he laughed. Personally, I did not think it was funny. He told me my mother had done her duty, and so had his mother, and that's why he and I were here. I just could not face Mrs. Moore.

About 10 a.m. Mrs. Moore came up to our room. Evan had been gone for hours helping his father on the farm. Stock still had to be fed and milked. Mrs. Moore was very nice. She talked to me and asked me to come down and eat something, but she let me know that breakfast was at a certain time, and if I wasn't there in the future, I would not be eating until lunch time. She made it sound like everything was okay. I guess it's a good thing Evan is leaving next week. Marriage will be a lot easier with no man around.

More Later,

Neaaka

February 3, 1942

*D*ear Ms. Diary,

Evan left last Sunday. It was nice to have the bed to myself. I guess I'm not a very good wife. I was sleeping so good at 4:30 this morning when Mrs. Moore came in and woke me. She said I had to go milk the cows. No one had said anything about that before. I didn't even know where the cows were. They had different barns.

I got dressed and took the pails and found two cows in one barn. I'd finished milking one and was getting ready to milk the second when Mr. Moore came in and asked what I was doing. I thought it was pretty obvious. I was milking a cow. He seemed very upset that Mrs. Moore had sent me out there. He said that was his job, and if I wanted to help, I could help the Mrs. in the kitchen. I wondered why she did that. Maybe I'll ask.

I went back into the house, and she was making breakfast. Mrs. Moore asked why I wasn't in the barn. When I told her Mr. Moore had sent me in to help her, she just scoffed. She was so sweet until Evan left. I'm not sure what happened. She told me if I thought I was going to lie around and do nothing, I'd better think again. I told her I would be glad to help her with whatever she needed me to do. She said I was being impertinent. I told her I would never do that. I had been taught to respect my elders. I swear I could almost see steam coming out of her ears.

I still don't know what I did to make her so mad. I noticed that her aprons were a little worn. I decided that when I got some material, I would make her a new one. Papa said when someone is not nice to you, do something good for them. It's the best way to get even, because they will feel guilty for treating you so bad. Boy, that lady has plenty of good coming her way. It's either that, or I'm going to slug her. Ms. Diary, I had not planned on writing you a whole lot, but we may both be in for a wild ride.

She asked if I could cook and was delighted to find out that I could. I explained that I had to teach myself, and I would be so grateful if she could teach me some more.

I found out she was worried about Evan going off to war. So I guess that might explain why she's not so nice right now. Evan told me he would have an allotment sent to me each month. He said it would be about eight dollars. I've never had that much money. I'm so excited. Ms. Diary, but let me tell you married life is not all it's cracked up to be. Night, Ms. Diary.

February 4, 1942

*D*ear Loretta,

It's been a while since I've written. Well, all I can say is stay single. Your life is not your own once you say, "I do".

Evan's been gone for more than a week now. I still don't have an address for him but should have one once he gets settled.

Loretta, I found out those wifely duties have nothing to do with housekeeping and farm chores. They are far worse. Of course, by the time Evan left, I didn't mind so much. It was kind of okay. I kicked Evan out of bed, and he hit the floor pretty hard the first night, but he didn't stay mad for very long.

Evan's papa is really nice. He told me to call him Cleve. And I call Mrs. Moore, Mrs. Moore. Cleve is much nicer.

I've always been told if you make an ugly face it might freeze and stay that way. I guess nobody told Mrs. Moore about that. Her face looks like stone. I have to keep saying, "I'm sorry Lord, I don't mean to judge."

I try to figure out how to please her, but then sometimes I do mean things. Like I watch her put something away, then I'll put it some totally crazy place to try and confuse her. Yesterday, she laid the milk-straining cloth on the table and went outside to the toilet. I took the cloth all wet and gooey and folded it and put it in the drawer with her dish towels. I felt bad for doing it, but I feel bad when she's not nice also. When she came back in, I was dusting the parlor, but I stood close enough to the door to watch her. She looked all around the kitchen for the straining cloth. She looked under the table and on top of everything. Then she said, "Neaaka, have you seen my straining cloth?"

I had to answer, "Yes." There was no way to get around it without lying, and I just couldn't do that. I told her it was lying on the table next to the dish towels she was folding before she went outside. That part was true. I hoped she wouldn't ask me anything else. I decided that being deceitful is just too much trouble, and it makes my belly hurt. So from here on out, I'm going to tell the truth just like it is. They can like it or not.

I'm up at 5:30 every morning. One day this past week, I cooked breakfast and let Mrs. Moore sleep in. She seemed appreciative. I've chopped wood, fed the chickens, gathered eggs, washed and ironed and even washed the woodwork. I've been very busy around here.

I would love to see my family, especially Luke and Levi.

I would love to wander into town and look around, but she keeps me so busy. Mr. Moore said I could ride into town with him sometime.

My sister Vonetta lives here in Sweet Run, but I've never been to her house. I'm afraid to invite her over without Mrs. Moore's permission.

I can't wait to tell my sister Kalinda what wifely duties are. She may decide to stay single forever.

My aunts Martha and Mabel are coming over soon. Maybe you could come with them. They are acquaintances of Mrs. Moore, so I'm sure it will be okay. I would love to see you. We could talk. I've got a whole lot to tell you.

I'll have to ask Mrs. Moore (Stone Face) for a stamp. "Sorry, Lord, she'll probably act like I'm asking for a hundred dollars. Lord, here I go again, put a bridle on my tongue. That's getting to be a big job."

I should be hearing from Evan any day now. I can

hardly wait. He's been gone a little over two weeks. I was sure I would have heard something by now. He asked me to write every day, and I said I would as soon as he sends me his address. I won't tell him how his mother is acting. We cannot worry our soldiers about trivial things back home. That's what everyone says.

I'm going to write Papa and Grandpa. I worry about them.

Well, I will close for now. Hope to see you soon.

Yours Truly,
Neaaka

February 11, 1942

*D*ear Papa and Grandpa,

It's been three weeks since I've left home. It seems a lot longer than that. How are you all doing? I really miss being there. I didn't think I would.

How are the boys doing? Papa, please be kind to them. They lost Momma and then me, and they are so little. I feel like a traitor, putting what I wanted above their welfare. I'm not at all sure I did the right thing. My bed is made, and I will lie in it to the best of my abilities.

How are you managing meals? Who's learning to cook, you or Grandpa?

I should hear from Evan any day now. I expected to hear before now, but maybe the mail is a little slower because of so many war letters.

Mrs. Moore keeps me busy all day long. I think she's using me for free labor. I don't mind helping out, but I feel like a maid. When bedtime comes, I'm so tired. I fall asleep instantly.

When the boys need new shirts, let me know, and I will make them some.

The owner of the feed store said he heard how pretty my wedding dress was and wondered if I would make one for his daughter. I'm meeting with her on Wednesday. She's coming here to talk with me. I've never done anything like this before. I'm a little scared. I guess that's how you learn.

Papa, I wish I was a little girl again, and Momma was still here. I miss her so much.

Is that ol' Ellie Parsons still hanging around? Papa I know you and the boys need someone, but does it have to be her?

I want to come home for a visit when the weather warms up. Maybe Cleve will let me borrow one of his horses, or maybe he will bring me in his truck. I've been thinking that maybe I would like to learn to drive. Mrs. Moore says women should not be doing things that are meant for men. I would just like to know who determines that men should drive and women shouldn't. I bet it was a man.

I made two aprons for Mrs. Moore. She barely said thank you. I don't get it. She was so nice before Evan left.

Papa, tell Luke, Levi, and Grandpa I said hello and hope to see them soon. I miss you all so much.

Much love and prayers,
Neaaka

February, 19, 1942

ear Ms. Diary,

I am so mad. I'm steaming again. I was helping Mrs. Moore with the wash today. I folded a load of her and Cleve's clothes and took them to their bedroom to lay them on the bed. I swear I didn't mean to snoop, but on the dresser was a stack of mail with my name on it. They were letters from Evan that I had been waiting on for weeks. That busybody! Can you believe it? She's been keeping Evan's letters from me. I ask her every day if there is any mail for me, and she tells me no. She waits out by the fence for the mailman to come. She's taking my letters and reading them. I feel sure that Evan is writing her also.

He's probably wondering why I haven't written to him. I'm so mad I can't even think straight.

I took the letters to my room and read them. Evan could not believe that I had not written to him. He thinks he made a mistake, and that I don't care about him. How am I going to fix this? I will just tell it like it is and let her deal with it. It would serve her right.

I'm going to wait until supper tonight to mention the letters. She's probably missed them by now. I want Mr. Moore to be there and see her face when she realizes I'm on to her. Cleve will not be happy, and neither am I. I should pray for her, but I am too mad right now. I'm trying to be a good Christian, but Lord it is so hard. Will you please kick the devil's butt and make him leave me alone? I'll try and do better.

More later, Ms. Diary

February, 12, 1942

*D*ear Ms. Diary,
Well you should have been there last night. It was so good. I helped Mrs. Moore with supper and acted like nothing was wrong. I think she knew I had

found the letters. Sometimes I would catch her looking at me like she was wondering what I was up to. I never let on.

We ate supper. Cleve and I made small talk and tried to include her. She wasn't interested at all. I told him about Mr. Dawson wanting me to make his daughter's wedding dress.

Mrs. Moore watched me from the corner of her eye.

When Cleve was about done eating, I asked Mrs. Moore if I'd gotten any mail from Evan. She told me no. She just bold-faced lied. I was not impressed. I asked her if she had received any mail from him since I hadn't. She stammered for a bit, then said why would she be getting letters from him when I was his wife. I stood up and held up the letters I had hidden in my apron pocket. I then told Cleve that these were letters from Evan to me, and I found them on their dresser. I glanced over at her, and I thought she was going to faint. Her face was without color. Her knees were so weak that she had to sit down. Cleve's face on the other hand had plenty of color, bright red to be exact. He got up and left the kitchen. He said he would be back in a few minutes. I had hoped he had gone out to get a switch.

She looked at me and said, "I hope you're happy now. See what you've done!"

I said, "No, why don't you tell me what I've done!"

She said I was snooping in her room. I couldn't help it. I laughed just a little.

Cleve was gone about ten minutes. He came in a lot calmer than he was when he left. He said, "Doris, Neaaka, sit down." We sat down and looked at each other wondering what was going to happen.

"Doris," he said, "Ever since Evan left you haven't treated Neaaka like a member of this family. You've worked her like she was your maid. You've been rude and self-serving like I've never known you to be. Neaaka has done everything you've asked her to do. She's even helped with outdoor chores. No matter what she does, she can't please you. Neaaka is still a child. She's not even sixteen years old yet. Yes, she is married to our son. Evan would be ashamed of you. You could have a daughter, but you've chosen to mistreat her. Why?"

Doris said, "She's not good enough for Evan. He should have married Sally Miller. She was much better suited to be Evan's wife. She's just trying to better herself and get out of that holler she was raised in. She'll never amount to a hill of beans. Evan could have done much better."

I sat there and said nothing. I just waited to see what was going to play out. Papa always said if you keep your mouth shut and your ears open, you'd be surprised what you can learn.

As I watched and listened to Mrs. Moore, I started to feel sorry for her. It's true I brought nothing to this marriage except myself. That's all I've got. I can learn if I had someone to teach me. I decided then to get an education. I would get books from the library and read as much as possible.

Cleve would not let us leave the table until we talked it out. I just love him. I asked Mrs. Moore why she didn't like me. She seemed to be taken aback that I was so direct in my question, but how else was I supposed to learn?

She said I was too young and didn't know what marriage was all about. I agreed with her and asked if she would teach me. I said if I'm not good enough for your son, then teach me. Make me good enough. She looked at me like it was the first time she'd ever seen me. I said, "Mrs. Moore, I waited for weeks to hear from Evan. I would have shared his letters with you. I'm not trying to take your son away from you. I thought we could be a family and do what's best for Evan. He's been sitting, God knows where, wondering why his wife has abandoned him. Letters are important to the soldiers, and Evan has never gotten one from me."

Mrs. Moore started to cry. She said she was sorry, and I truly believe she was. She said Evan's going away was my fault, but as soon as she said it she knew it wasn't true. It just wore me out last night to have to share my feelings. This is not what I do best. I will have a tough time sleeping. Maybe tomorrow will be a better day.

Greta Dawson is coming by to talk about her wedding dress. I made a few sketches. I'm going to write Evan so many letters today he will think I've got diarrhea of the pen. I will read the letters from Evan again before I answer them. We'll probably talk again tonight.

Later Ms. Diary

February 14, 1942

Dear Neaaka,
I just got here, and I'm getting settled. I can't wait to hear from you and find out what's going on. How are you getting on with my family? They're very sweet people and will treat you nice. I hope you are helping around the house.

Neaaka, I've heard terrible stories since I've been here about the Germans gathering up the Jews and putting them somewhere called Auschwitz or something like that. They say they are killing them. I cannot imagine one human being doing that to another. There will probably be some things blacked out in some of my letters if I say something I shouldn't about the war effort.

They tell us that on December 19 some guy named Hitler assumed the position of post commander in chief of the German Army. A few weeks before I got here, the German U-boats began sinking ships just off the American coast in Operation Drumbeat. It's getting real bad, Neaaka. The only thing I'm sure of is I'm coming home to you come hell or high water. Please be there for me.

You'll be getting your allotment check real soon. I don't have a lot of time. We have to get up at five every morning. It's still very cold outside. I've been told that my platoon will ship out the second week of April. I don't know where to, and when I do, I may not be able to tell you. I may get to come home on furlough for a few days. Sure hope so anyway. I'm sending you my address, please don't lose it.

How are Mom and Dad doing? I got a letter from Mom, but she didn't mention you. I'm surprised I haven't heard from you. Mom has my address from where I wrote to her the same time I wrote to you. I'm getting real worried.

My address is:

Thomas Evan Moore 415669
Division 13
APO, 669 Great Falls, Montana

Neaaka, please hurry and write to me. I'd love to get a letter from you before I ship out. That's kind of strange, isn't it? You used to get on my nerves by writing so much, and now I can't wait to hear from you. Honey, write real soon.

Hugs and kisses,
Your husband,
Evan

February 18, 1942

*D*ear Neaaka,
I've been gone three weeks and still haven't heard from you. What's going on? Have you found someone else? I guess that's a soldier's greatest fear. I've only been gone a short while, so I'm assuming that's not the case. Honey, this letter is going to be short. I'm trying to get a few words down before the lights go out.

I heard that in January a German by the name of Rommel ran counterattacks on the Americans in North Africa. I didn't even know we had Americans in Africa. It's probably not safe to say a lot, but at the same time I will be learning also. I've met some real nice young men from all over America. Some I think will be very good friends. The lights are going out in two minutes.

Write soon,
Love and miss you,
Evan

March 2, 1942

*D*ear Loretta,

I must be the world's most terrible person. Mrs. Moore's brother came over today, but for some reason he makes me so uncomfortable. I've seen him at church many times over the years. He always seemed like a nice enough man, but I just have this bad feeling when he is around. He has never done anything to me or said anything out of the way. Sometimes I catch him looking at me out of the corner of his eye. When I see him do that, he looks away real quick as if he has been caught with his hand in the cookie jar.

Loretta, I don't really like being married. It might be different if Evan were here, or I were home with my family. Doris is not a pleasant person to be around all the time. She does have her moments though.

I am reading her books. Sometimes I think I could write like that, but I only have an eighth-grade education, I guess there's not a whole lot you can do with that. I hated school, so I sure have no intention of going again.

Loretta, do you think God has our lives all planned out, and there's nothing we can do to change it, or do you think he just gives us the tools, you know, like common sense, a brain, a body that works, and expects us to figure out what to do with everything?

Grandpa always says the Lord provides everything we need. I used to think he meant food and shelter. I now think he means literally everything.

I think I'm smart, especially when it comes to reading people and figuring them out. I guess I was wrong though about old poker face Ellie. She seems nice enough now that I know her a little better. She seems to really like my little brothers. How could anyone help it though? They are so cute. I really miss them. I'm afraid they will think I abandoned them, and maybe, in a way, I did.

Loretta, write and tell me all about yourself. Sometimes when I read back what I wrote to you, I feel like a whiny butt. It must be exciting to live in a small town and get to see different people every day. I live here with the Moores now, but on a farm no one comes around much.

Loretta, I'm not one to distrust or not like anyone without a reason. Why do you think I have such negative feelings for Evan's Uncle Wilbert? It really bothers me. If

I'm going to dislike someone, I would really like to have a reason.

I am so glad we are friends. It's good to have someone to talk to about things. I talk to you and "Ms. Diary." I tell her everything. I hope she never tells anyone on me. I would be in so much trouble.

I will close for now. Mrs. Moore and Cleve are going into town tomorrow and I'm going to do the laundry. It will be my first time to do it here all by myself, however, I have helped her with it.

Write to me real soon. I so enjoy getting letters in the mail.

Best regards,
Neaaka

March, 4, 1942

Dear Neaaka,
What the hell is going on? I'm trying real hard to not get mad. Why haven't you written to me? Mom is writing real often, why aren't you? When I didn't want you to write, you wrote all the time.

I can't believe you decided to stop and never write to

me again. I'm not mad, really, just frustrated. It's lonely not being home and in familiar surroundings. Please forgive me. I'm sure there's a sensible explanation.

Write soon,

Love,

Evan

March 16, 1942

*D*ear Evan,
  I am so sorry for not writing sooner, there was a mix up with the mail. Your mom accidently laid the mail on her dresser and forgot to give it to me. I don't think she will let that happen again.

I'm glad you are meeting some nice young men.

Evan, most of the time, I want to go back home and live with Papa and Grandpa. I know I couldn't wait to get out of there, but I miss them and my little brothers.

I listen to the radio every evening. It makes more sense now than it used to. I must be growing up. Your Mom keeps me pretty busy, and I've been sewing quite a bit.

Evan please write again soon. I want to know everything about what you do and the people you meet. It sounds so exciting to get to see the world and meet lots of different people. When you come home, do you think we could travel to some beautiful paradise? I don't really know what paradise is, but I'm sure it is wonderful. We could see new sights and sounds and fill our hearts with joy. Evan, I will write again tomorrow.

Much love and prayers,
Neaaka

March 17, 1942

*D*ear Evan,
I've read all your letters again and again. I'm sorry you got so upset. Please know I will never look at another man. When I married you, it was for a lifetime if you can put up with me that long. I'm a little hard-headed, and you can't fix that, but maybe you can learn to live with it. Ha, ha.

Your papa is planting some early potatoes today. I offered to go help him, but he said no. So I washed the breakfast dishes for your mom.

Spring is starting to come to life. I love it when I start to see little green shoots on the branches and things poking their heads out of the ground after a long hard winter. Evan, I hope this finds you well and not too awfully homesick. I'm sure this crazy war will be over, and we can be together soon. In the meantime, I pray for you every night. I know in my heart you are coming home.

Write real soon,

Neaaka

April 10, 1942

*D*ear Ms. Diary,

I don't like Uncle Wilbert. He's a creepy old man, always sneaking around. Let me tell you about him. I hope Evan never reads you, or I will be in real trouble. Uncle Wilbert is a short, fat, balding man. He always looks like he needs a shave. He lets the back of his hair grow longer than looks good. I assume that if he can't grow it on top, he will grow it wherever he can. His eyes are narrow, green, and squinty. He always looks like he needs a haircut but is too lazy to get one.

Uncle Wilbert gives me the creeps. Sometimes I catch him looking at me through his squinty eyes. It makes me feel as if I need to take a bath, but since it isn't Saturday, I won't.

Everyone always talks about what a good man Uncle Wilbert is, and I have no reason to think otherwise. It is just a feeling I get. I guess I just don't understand these feelings. I've never had them before.

I remember he came and helped Mr. Sansom with the barn raising. One time when Mr. Dawson was under the weather, he helped him get his crops in. I guess, as a friend and neighbor, he has a good reputation. However, I am always glad he's Evan's uncle and not mine.

Yesterday, when the Moores were gone and I was home by myself, Uncle Wilbert came by. I told him his sister and Cleve had gone into town. I was hanging out wash. My sister Vonnie had bought me a pair of silk underwear when I got married, and that was the last thing I needed to hang on the line. I stopped and tried to make small talk because I just couldn't hang my new silk underwear up in front of him. I told him it would be a while, and maybe he could come back later.

He said no he would just stick around, from where he was standing the view was just fine. I didn't know what he was talking about. It was the same old hills and creeks he always seen when he was there. It took a few minutes for me to realize he wasn't looking at the view around him but was staring at me. I told him I had work to do and excused myself. I left my underwear in the bushel basket that we used for laundry thinking I would just lay it across something in my room to dry. He asked me if I was going to hang up that pretty pink thing in the basket. I told him no, that it would be fine. I said, "You need to leave, because of all your yammering I haven't been able to finish my work."

I started back towards the house and realized he was following me. I knew I had to stay outside, because no one was around anywhere.

I prayed Doris and Cleve would come back early.

As I stepped upon the porch, I spotted a shotgun standing in the corner that Cleve filled with buckshot to scare unwanted animals away. I sat down next to the gun and hoped he would go away. He was Evan's mother's brother. They were a nice family. I couldn't figure out what was wrong with me. This man had never done anything to me. Just a feeling, that's all it is. Get over it, Neaaka.

Wilbert sat down in the chair next to me, and we pretended to make small talk. I just wanted him to leave. He reached down into the basket and picked up my silk panties and said, "Whew, I sure would like to see you in these."

I grabbed the shotgun and fired over his head, but one of the buckshot struck him in the forehead. You never heard such cussing and carrying on. While he was still in shock, I reloaded the gun from a box Cleve had left sitting on the porch bannister beside the gun. I said, "You need to leave, and you only come back here when Doris and Cleve are home, and if you don't leave right now, I'm going to fill your hind end full of buckshot."

His head was bleeding a little from the buckshot wound, and he pulled a handkerchief from the pocket of his dirty overalls and started wiping blood from over his eye. "Girl, you could have put my eye out!"

"Then you would have had one less eye to ogle me with," I retorted angrily. Just then Doris and Cleve pulled up in their truck.

Til tomorrow,
Neaaka

April 13, 1942

*D*ear Neaaka,
It is always a pleasure to receive your letters. I can tell by the way you write you are very smart, and I believe you could do or be anything you want. I think

you would make a good seamstress. I saw the way you tackled making your brothers some shirts and didn't give up until you got it right. You seem like you like to sew.

You can do so many things, like cook and can and whatever needs to be done. Your momma taught you well. My momma says it's easier to just do things herself rather than teach me. I'm taking a page from your book and starting to teach myself things I want to know. I'm reading more, and one day I looked through the dictionary to try and learn some new words, but all it did was show me how much I did not know. I found it overwhelming. I bet you would have said I can do this, because I know you try to learn a new word every day and the meaning. I admire you for that.

I just always thought I would get married and let my husband take care of me. Lately though, I've been having dreams of my own. With the war going on, I think I may get a job or something. It doesn't seem right to just do nothing.

Your Aunt Mabel gave me two more sewing lessons, but I do not like to sew enough to keep it up. If I want something made, maybe I can get you to do it for me.

There aren't many guys around to choose from for a husband. Neaaka, do you think I might be an old maid? I'm almost eighteen, most girls are married by now, and some even have a baby. I feel left out sometimes. My momma says I'm being silly, and that when the time is right, the Lord will work it out. I guess I should be more trusting.

I will write again.

As always,
Loretta

April 12, 1942

*D*ear Ms. Diary,
Why does life have to be so difficult? Today I was home alone. Mr. and Mrs. Moore went into town, and I stayed behind to catch up on writing to Evan. Mrs. Moore's brother Wilbert came by. He's a creepy old man, and he still scares me. He came in, and I was trying to be a good hostess. I offered him some coffee, but it was cold, and he said no, but there was something he would like to have. All the while he was grinning that evil grin at me. We were standing in front of the fireplace, and he reached out and grabbed my breast. I grabbed the poker from the fireplace and hit him across the upper arm, and he fell over a table. While he was cursing and getting up, I pulled Cleve's double-barreled shotgun off the wall and loaded both chambers. By the time he got up, I was

pointing the gun at him and told him to leave and never come back when I'm here.

He said, "This is my sister's house, and I'll come here whenever I take a notion."

"Well, I have a notion to split your bag and run your leg through it. You jolly well better believe it's not a threat."

He looked at me with that evil grin. By then I had moved closer to the front door. He said, "You're just a little girl from the head of some holler, what do you know about shooting a shotgun?"

Luckily the window was open, and as the pellets passed by his left leg he turned so white he looked like a ghost. He had a little trouble getting traction to get out of there. Just as he cleared the gate, I shot the fence post beside him. I've never seen an old man move so fast in my whole life.

So now I have to explain why part of the fence post is missing, and the dirt is dug up outside the window. I thought I would make something up. But it's too much trouble to lie, so I guess I will tell them the truth. Mrs. Moore is not going to be happy, and she will say I'm lying. But we'll see what happens.

Ms. Diary, I hear Cleve's truck coming, and I have not written to Evan yet. Sure can't tell him about his Uncle Wilbert.

Cleve got out of the truck and looked at the fence post and then at me on the porch. By now I had set the gun down on the porch. Doris didn't notice it. They walked by me and spoke and took some things into the house. Cleve said nothing. I thought he was so mad that he was waiting a while to talk to me because that's his way. A few minutes later he came out on the porch and sat down on the swing. He said, "Missy, I noticed some things upset in the house. Care to tell me what happened?"

I said, "No, I don't care to tell you, but Doris is going to be mad."

He decided he'd better have Doris come out because she thought I was just clumsy and didn't have the decency to clean up my mess. I explained about her brother and what he had done. She called me a little tramp and said it was my fault, that I must have done something to make him do such a thing. I didn't say anything bad about her brother. I let her talk and Cleve watched me watch her. I could tell he was glad I was keeping my mouth shut. She said her son had married a slut, and she was sure she had been right, that he had married beneath him. I was seething mad, but I kept quiet for Cleve's sake. She finished her little speech and walked back in the house and slammed the door.

I said, "Cleve, you don't believe me either, do you?"

He said, "Yes, Missy, I do, and Doris will too when she has time to think about it. It's not the first time someone has accused him of inappropriate actions. Neaaka, as long as I've known you I've never known you to lie. There have been times when lying would have been easier, but you stood up and took what was coming to you and never blamed anyone else. So yes, I believe you."

I couldn't believe what I was hearing. I love Cleve; he is such a good man. I knew that old Uncle Wilbert was not a good person.

I stood there trying to get my nerve up so I could go in and help Doris with supper if she will let me in the kitchen. She had her back to me, but said, "I hope you're happy."

I replied, "I was until your creepy brother came over." Oops, I was going to keep my mouth shut.

She turned around, and there were tears in her eyes. "I'm sorry," she said and walked away.

I finished supper, we ate, but all the small talk was strained. I went to bed and decided that not only is Wilbert a creep, he is also a hypocrite, pretending to be a worthy deacon in the church. I hope he stays away from me. I might not be so nice next time.

I've been a little queasy at my stomach today. Tomorrow must be a better day.

Night Ms. Diary. We'll talk later.

April 14, 1942

*D*ear Loretta,

I think I'm losing my mind. Doris sat me down Saturday and told me she thinks I'm going to have a baby. Don't you think that's the craziest thing you ever heard of? I only had a husband for one week, and then he was gone. She said she knew because I have not had my monthly and am beginning to show. I told her it was just her good cooking.

Loretta, do you know how people have a baby? I've been trying to figure it out ever since she told me I was going to. She said it happens when two people come together such as a husband and wife. Then I remembered the morning after my wedding. Do you think it could have happened then?

I was thinking about getting my own place if I could sew and make enough money, but, if I am going to have a baby, I may have to stay here. I started thinking about a little Evan and got excited. Doris said I should feel it move soon. What could it possibly be like to feel another person move inside your body? I think Doris has made a big mistake.

Cleve has been giving me driving lessons, and so far

I've managed to stay out of the creek. I drove over to the feed store on Tuesday. Of course, Cleve was with me. Doris still thinks a woman has no business driving anything, even a team of mules.

Aunt Mabel came over, and I showed her Greta Dawson's material and the design I had worked up. She seemed surprised that I could do that. She said it would be the talk of the town. From what I gather, the whole town is invited. Aunt Mabel is coming back over in a couple of days. I will ask her if she thinks I'm "big." She's going to help me with the dress.

I started getting an allotment from Evan. I've never had money before. At first I wanted to go to town and just buy everything. I soon figured out that would be wasteful. So I'll save as much as possible, and when Evan comes home, maybe we can buy a farm somewhere. Loretta, it's late, and I'll have to finish up tomorrow.

Aunt Mabel came over today instead of tomorrow and I asked her if she thought I was "big."

She looked me up and down and said, "Well, you're bigger than you were last time I saw you," and laughed. Doris had already told her I was going to have a baby. It makes me mad that everyone else knew before me.

We got a lot done on the dress. By tomorrow evening it should be ready for Greta to try on. It won't be finished of course, but when we make a few adjustments, it will be.

Next time Aunt Mabel comes over, why don't you come with her? I would love to see you. Aunt Mabel asked me what I was going to name the baby. How could I think of names for a baby when I just learned that there was going to be one? Sometimes I imagine that it's all in their heads.

I started out to the barn today to take Biscuit for a ride, and Doris stopped me. She said I should not be riding the pony while I was in my condition. What condition? It makes no sense to me at all, and the only reason I'm paying any attention to her at all is because my momma told me I should listen to my elders. Lord knows she is one of those. Well, I've rambled on and on tonight. It usually doesn't take me two days to write a letter. Maybe I'm slowing down because I'm "big." I still have to write Evan tonight. Do you think I should tell Evan I'm going to have a baby or just let him be surprised like I was? I guess now I know what condition Doris was talking about.

Loretta, I get so lonely here with just Doris and Cleve. I should make myself go over to Vonnie's. I don't know how long it will take before Cleve trusts me with the truck. I've got a pretty good handle on the clutch now. I don't kill the engine near as often as I used to. I probably could make it to Vonnie's. She just lives about three miles from me.

Good night and sleep tight, Loretta.

Yours truly,
Neaaka

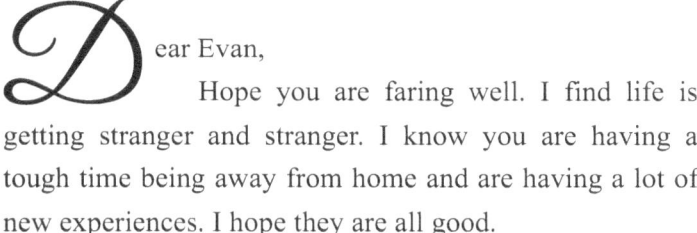

April, 1942

*D*ear Evan,

Hope you are faring well. I find life is getting stranger and stranger. I know you are having a tough time being away from home and are having a lot of new experiences. I hope they are all good.

I'm having a few new experiences myself, or at least your mom says I am, I don't know. Evan, she looked me right in the eye and told me I was going to have a baby. I told her no I wasn't, and she grinned that silly little grin (sorry I know she's your mother), and said women have a way of knowing these things, Well, fiddlesticks, I'm a woman and I didn't know.

The only reason I believe her is because she insisted I go see Doc Green, and he told me I was going to have a baby. Evan, I've almost never been so embarrassed. He made me get up on a table, and well, I can't even tell you what he did to me.

How could he tell there was a baby in there? I kept asking how, and could he see it. He said, "No, he could just tell." He said I was three months along. That means the baby will be here in October. He said if you take the first day of your last period and count back three months, then add seven days, and that would be the due date. So according to him our baby is due on October 23rd.

I just hate when your mom is right. She told me it was very painful to have a baby, but I figure it couldn't hurt any worse than rolling down the hill through a briar patch and landing under an old log. I guess we will talk more about this later.

I have been listening to the radio a lot more lately. It's kind of funny that only two years ago I hated the news. I got so tired of Grandpa always wanting to hear it and getting upset about a war that had not even happened. Evan, I never dreamed that you would be part of the news someday. Your mom is nicer to me now than she used to be. I think she likes the idea of a new baby coming. She says we are going to make a layette. I am kind of excited about that. I could design baby clothes. Maybe I could sell them, and we would get rich. Oh well, it never hurts to dream.

I'm going over to Vonnie's Sunday afternoon. We will probably talk about you and her old man. That doesn't sound very nice, but that's what she calls him. I'm sure it's all done in love because I know she adores him. Vonnie's baby is due the end of July. Maybe she'll let me get in a little practice before our baby gets here. I am going to be Aunt Neaaka at sixteen. I have a birthday next month so I will actually be sixteen. Wow, I'm getting so old!

Evan, I rambled on and on, but I want you to know I think about you all the time and about what our lives will be like when you get home. I know horrible things are happening during the war, and I hope you are shielded from most of them. My uncle Ronald fought in WWI, and the war changed him. Evan, please don't let the war change you. I don't think I could bear it.

I'm saving the allotment check so we can buy our own place when you get back. Maybe if I get enough saved and find a place nearby, I can go ahead and buy it and surprise you when you come home. Then all you would have to do is get some horses and a plow, and we would be in business.

There's another girl in town who wants me to make her wedding dress. She saw Greta Dawson's and loved it. I've been working on some sketches. Your mom said my sketches were disgraceful and showed too much skin. I think your mom is old-fashioned, so I'll wait and see what this girl thinks. Her name is Artabelle.

Evan, I try and think good thoughts about you and pray for your safe return.

Will you write and tell me about some of the guys in your outfit and what kind of food you eat and how you sleep? I want to know how things are with you so I can imagine how you make it through each day.

I will write again tomorrow. Cleve is going to let me take the truck into town to meet Artabelle and show her my sketches. I'll tell you all about it. Last time he let me take the truck I had a flat and drove it all the way home. I didn't know you were supposed to fix it before you drove it. Anyway, I didn't know how, but now I do. Cleve helped me fix it and showed me what to do in case it ever happened again. Doris acted like I was stupid. I guess I was. We never owned a vehicle.

Doris has already started on the layette for the baby. She is wasting no time. She has already made three little dresses. She said little boys wore dresses too. I remember Luke and Levi wore them when they were little. I guess it will be all right.

Evan, I love you and miss you and pray for you. Write soon.

Your ever loving wife,

Neaaka

April 30, 1942

Dear Neaaka,

A baby! We're going to have a baby. I can hardly believe it. I want to come home so bad. I miss you. I'm always so glad to hear from home. I'm now in Rome, N.Y. It's very cold here. This is a new base, but it's unfinished. The mud is knee deep. Every time I walk across the base to the chow hall I think I may drown in the mud.

Our shoes have to be shined. It's very hard to keep things clean. I'm a private first class, and my boss told me it will be very easy to rise in rank right now with the war going on. I'm going to try and make sergeant as soon as I can. That will mean a raise in pay. I guess, with a baby coming, we will need it.

It would be so nice if you could send me that little RCA radio on the shelf in our room. We have no way of hearing the news except what our commanding officers tell us. You can take it over to Ed's radio shop and have it checked out. Be sure it has a good battery.

I bet you're looking good right now and getting a little bigger. As I write this and the news is sinking in, I'm getting excited about the baby. Have you thought of any names yet? I like Cleveland after my dad if it's a boy.

I've been working in the supply room, and it's okay. It's not real hard work. I need to figure out how to stream-line getting supplies in and out more efficiently. I had one day of KP, that's kitchen duty. One day was enough, and I never want to do that again. They should have some women in the kitchen doing women's work. It was very degrading, a man doing women's work.

My commanding officer is very hard-nosed about

things. I think he could get more done if he were a bit nicer.

Neaaka, I hope my mom is still being nice to you. I couldn't believe she was short with you. I guess that's a side of her I didn't know. I appreciate you not saying anything about her to me. I've been reading between the lines in her letters. I can't imagine anyone not loving you. I was so blind for so long. You are a wonderful person with a big heart. I can't wait until this war is over, and I can come home to you and our baby.

I will be going overseas soon. I hope I can come home for a few days before I leave.

I would like to buy a farm for us to live on and raise our family. How does that sound to you?

Pete Withrow and I hitchhiked into town last weekend. We had supper and saw a movie. It was nice. I had never seen a moving picture show before. I guess I'm in for a lot of new experiences.

Funny thing, you can get a ride anywhere if you have a uniform on.

How's Biscuit doing? I know you and Dad are taking good care of him.

Have you finished that girl's wedding dress yet? I know it will be very pretty. You're so talented.

Well, will close for now. If you get a letter sometime and some of it is blacked out, you'll know I wrote something that I shouldn't have. I don't think that will happen for a while. I'll write again soon.

Write and tell me some names you are thinking of, and I'll tell you some things I'm thinking of. I guess Doris for a girl would be out of the question. Ha, ha.

I will have to make sure my shoes are mud free for morning inspection.

All my love,
Evan

May 8, 1942

D ear Loretta,

I haven't had time to write for a while. Things have really been busy here. I have been helping Cleve with the planting as much as he will let me. I help Dad and Grandpa, too. I really enjoy putting a plant in the ground and knowing it will provide food just like the good Lord intended. We are so blessed.

We start breakfast around five. I sometimes wonder what it would be like to sleep until I wanted to get up. I've never done that. Even as a child there was breakfast to eat on time and chores to be done. I don't ever remember sleeping until I wanted to get up. I guess that sounds pretty lazy doesn't it?

I am so tired lately. By the time supper is over and the animals are fed, I'm ready to fall asleep, but I can't because that's when I sew. I'm trying to figure out how to fit a baby into my busy schedule, but other people do it, and I know I can do anything anybody else can do.

I design and make my own clothes since I've gotten "big." Doris said she had never heard of such a thing as having special clothes for having a baby, but it makes sense to me. I won't be this size forever I hope. I'm really beginning to fill out, but I'm only four months along. I'm very surprised at how far the skin will stretch; it must have a limit. I wonder if anyone has ever just burst before their baby got here. Vonnie's baby is due at the end of July. She's stretching pretty far.

I've been thinking about names. Evan wants to name it Cleveland if it's a boy. I love Cleve dearly; I don't like his name, however. I can come up with lots of boys names, but am having trouble with girls' names. I thought I might name a girl Nyoka after my mom, but it's a ways off. I may change my mind many times. I often do. I've written Evan and asked him if he had any suggestions. Cleveland was the only one I got so far.

Enough about me. Aunt Martha told me you were going to school. I am glad you are, however, I'm glad I don't have to anymore. I still like to learn, but that's something I can do on my own. At school the kids really hurt my feelings. They called me *Injun* and *half-breed*. Momma told me they were ignorant, and I know that, but it didn't make it hurt any less. There was one boy who was good to me and took up for me. His name was Enos.

There were a couple of girls, also. One was Betty Caldwell, and the other was Shirley Jeffers. I think I will always remember them. Shirley's family moved away about four years ago. I'm so glad I don't have to go back to school anymore.

Have you completely given up on sewing? Aunt Martha or Aunt Mabel can show you how, but you really just have to tackle it and figure it out for yourself.

Do you have another boyfriend yet? You really don't need one, unless of course, you really want one. What are you studying? I hope it is something very interesting.

They are having a scrap drive on Saturday down at the courthouse. Cleve is gathering up all kinds of metal to take down. He brought Evan's old bicycle down from the barn. I hope Evan is done with it. He used to ride it over to Papa's to see me. I wanted to try and ride it myself, but Doris and Cleve acted like I was going to commit some big sin.

I will be glad not to be "big" any more. I've got five more months to go. That seems like forever. I wonder what it will be like to have another whole little person to take with me wherever I go. I hope I like doing that.

As always,
Neaaka

June 4, 1942

*D*ear Neaaka,

I got your letter on Tuesday. I've been thinking about girls' names for you. Your sisters are Alice, Vonetta, and Kalinda. Maybe you would want to use one of their names. I'm sure they would be pleased. I also like Isabella, Rosa, Céline, and Eileen. I won't be offended if you don't use any of them. I'm just trying to help. I really like Nyoka after your momma. Oh well, I'm sure you and Evan will come up with a beautiful name for a boy or a girl, but I really love Isabella and you could call her Belle.

Yes, Martha and Mabel both gave me several sewing lessons. I made an apron and a straight-line skirt. I haven't tackled a blouse yet. That may be next on the list.

I have decided I want to learn to drive. I think if you can, I can too. With the war and all, you never know when it will be necessary. My Dad does not have a car or truck and with gas rationing, it may be awhile.

There is a young man over at the bank that I like very much. He is an only child and his mom and dad are both dead. He lives with his grandparents and helps take care of them. He didn't have to go into the service because he is their only support. He really wanted to go and do his part, but felt he had to be here, also. He seems real nice and he's not bad to look at either. He's coming over Saturday evening, and we are going to walk into town. That's all Mom will let me do.

I've heard you talk about keeping a diary and thought I would try it. It's nice to look back on. It's amazing how many little details you forget until you read them again.

I'm so sorry you had such a hard time in school. My momma says that when people say things like that, there is something lacking in their life. I kind of believe that. I know you are very smart and you will go far if you want.

I will write to you again in a few days and let you know how my date went.

As always,
Loretta

June 6, 1942

*D*ear Neaaka,
They finally got some boardwalks made, but the mud is still bad.

I'm working full time in supplies now and like it very much. It's easy work, and I don't have to spend much time marching and other things.

I can't wait until I can come home. I'm anxious to read your diary and find out what your secrets are. I bet they're doozies.

Rumor has it that we're shipping out by the end of the month. They had told us earlier that it would be April, but that didn't happen. That means I won't be in the states when the baby comes.

My CO says I'm doing an exemplary job in the warehouse. He tells me I should move up fast through the ranks but nothing yet.

I've been meaning to ask what you're doing with the allotment. I know you said you were saving it. If you want to give Mom and Dad a little extra along the way, I guess that would be okay.

I've been thinking about names for the baby. It's hard when you think a child is going to be stuck with its name for the rest of its life. Dad never really liked his name. We should choose a name that he or she will be proud of. Maybe we could name a boy after a president or someone famous. I thought about Samuel after your papa. I like the names Franklin, Roy, Jacob, Eli, Michael, Gabriel, and Paul. For a girl I like Marlene, Marilyn, Isabella, and JoAnn. I'm going to leave the naming to you. I know you'll think it out and do a good job.

Well honey, I have to go to bed and rest for tomorrow.

Write soon, I love you and can't wait to see you.

Love,
Evan

July 5, 1942

*D*ear Evan,
Do you ever daydream? Sometimes I do. I think of faraway places, and in my mind they are beautiful. Someday, I would like to travel.

I was very extravagant this past week. I went into town with Cleve and bought a *Life* and a *Post* magazine. I know twenty cents is a lot to spend on something so frivolous. It's just that they seemed to have so much to say. I saw a lot of magazines with women's clothing in them, but I was content with the two I had.

There is so much to learn, I feel like I may explode if I don't learn everything. I have read the magazines cover to cover twice. If I'm not too tired tonight, I may read them again. I am also reading your mother's books on the shelf in the parlor. I especially love her poetry book by Emily Dickinson. Someday I may write a poem for you.

It's July, and some of the gardening stuff is coming in,

like tomatoes and cucumbers. I guess we will be making pickles and canning tomatoes for a month or so. The end of the crops will be in August.

Vonnie's baby is due at the end of this month. I can't wait. She already knows what she wants to name it. She is so big, and the weather is so hot, she says sometimes she just wants to stick her head in the creek and let the cool water run over it. I told her that could be a problem, and she just laughed. We enjoy our time together. It's kind of nice being grown-up sisters.

I helped Momma a lot when it was canning time. It gives you such a good feeling to look in the cellar and see all the food you have preserved for winter. Blackberries are ripe now also, but Doris and Cleve won't let me pick any. Being big with child sure gets in the way sometimes. I can't ride Biscuit, and can't pick berries, can't do this, and can't do that. I'll be glad when the baby gets here; I'm going to let it do whatever it wants.

I've been designing and making my own "big" clothes. I get compliments on them. A couple of ladies asked me to make an outfit each for their daughters who are expecting. They had their own feed sacks and are going to bring them to me. I really like sewing and making clothes. Mrs. Robinson, down at the general store, said I should make a dress and put it in her store with my name on a card, and maybe I could get some orders, and she could sell some material. It sounded like a good idea to me, so I did and now have another two orders. I work on them at night so as to not interfere with the daily chores.

Evan, I don't know where in this big world you are. Are you on a ship? Are you in a foreign country? Are you fighting and killing people? Are you working in another warehouse somewhere? I imagine you in all kinds of situations and pray for you to return home to us.

I would like to send you some blackberry jam and things if it would be all right with your CO. Let me know.

At least you don't have to deal with the mud any more. I know there are some things you can't tell me, but please write and tell me what you can even if some of it is blacked out, maybe I can read between the lines.

Evan, I'm saving the money that I get from sewing and putting it in with my allotment. I only use it to buy sewing supplies to make more money. It's adding up quite nicely. I've got $92.60.

I think I have already told you that Mr. Dawson's son is missing. They have had no word on him for five weeks now. As you can imagine, they are heartsick, and who can blame them?

It's so nice that you're meeting lots of other young men from different parts of the country. I think that's exciting, although the circumstances are not.

I have not heard from Papa, Grandpa, and the boys for a couple of weeks. I will go over to visit them soon. I'm sure your papa won't mind my taking the truck. He might even go with me. He and Grandpa will get along great.

The boys will be so excited to see a little Evan or a little Neaaka. I hope the baby looks like you. I've decided on a girl's name, so you are going to be surprised. I hope you like it.

Honey, it's getting late, and I still have a lot to do, so will close for now. I looked at a big world map at the general store Saturday and tried to figure where you are but no luck. The world is too big.

Just waiting for the time you can come home and we can be a family.

I am anxiously waiting to hear from you. I'll check the mailbox every day.

Loving and missing you. Come home soon.

Much love,
Neaaka

July 7, 1942

*D*ear Neaaka,

Another day of duty, and that's exactly what it is because if it wasn't my duty, I wouldn't be doing it. I'd be home with you.

Most evenings I'm too tired to think, but I always think

of you and our baby. You're a good woman, Neaaka. I know you are very young, but you're older than your years.

After supper tonight, we gathered for some board games to help us relax. They had some geography quizzes, states and capitals quizzes, and some spelling and math challenges. I believe school would have been much more enjoyable if we'd been able to learn like this by playing games rather than the rote method. Then we gathered around the radio for an update on the war news. The reporters were positive in reporting, making us all sound good. We heard that seven destroyers had been sunk in the last engagement.

I've met some real nice young men from all over the U.S. They're just like me. I've always wondered what people were like in different parts of the country. Turns out, there are no differences at all. I guess God made us all pretty much alike.

Charlie Hager and I, along with lots of others, stood in line for three hours to get paid on Wednesday. A few of us are getting a weekend pass to go into town. I can't tell you the name of the town, We are going to have dinner and take in a movie.

I was so sorry to hear about Mr. Dawson's son. He was a nice young man. He may be all right. He might be in a place where he can't get a letter out. Please give Mr. Dawson my best wishes.

I've been going to clerical school for the last three days

now studying company administration. That's records to keep personnel straight. It's very complicated.

I wish I could see a picture of you. Do you know anyone with a camera?

Have you decided on a name for a boy yet? I trust you to choose a good one. I'm sure Mom will help you with the baby, and Dad will help you spoil it.

I'm anxious for some real soldiering. I realize keeping track of supplies is a very important job, but I'd like to do something a little more manly.

Neaaka, if you save enough from your sewing and allotment to buy a little farm I think that would be very nice.

How are your papa and brothers doing? I wish I had gotten to know them before I left. They will all be anxious to see the baby.

Joe Ellis, a guy from Montana, came into the rec room today, and a cardboard cutout of Uncle Sam fell over. Joe just looked at it and said, "My dad said if I ever enlisted, Uncle Sam would fall over. Reckon he was right." He walked on down into the sleeping quarters, and the whole rec room full of men laughed, but Joe never cracked a smile. There are some funny things that happen around here.

A lot of the men here end up with nicknames. I don't have one yet, but it could happen any day. One guy from Georgia is called "The Rock." I don't know why yet. One is called "Too Tall Jones." He's about 6' 6". Most of us guys are around 5' 10" or so.

I guess Vonnie's baby is due any day now. I know you are all excited. Just think, in a few months it will be our turn.

I love you so much, Neaaka. I need a picture of you to keep in my hat so when I get lonesome for you I can take it out and look at it.

Babe, I will go for now. It'll be lights out before I know it.

I'm going to dream of you and the baby and our little farm. I'm saving some money also. I will send it home when I can. It's not much, but every little bit helps.

Write soon. I can't wait to get your letters. It's like a breath of fresh air. I love you very much. Maybe absence does make the heart grow fonder.

Much love,

Evan

July 12, 1942

*D*ear Evan,

Vonnie had her baby last Friday. It was a little boy. She named him James Samuel after Jim and Papa. He's beautiful. I'm not sure you're supposed to say that about a boy. Maybe I should just say he is handsome.

Evan, you never say anything about where you're at or what country you are in. I remember seeing the big world map in Mrs. Halstead's classroom and at the general store. I think about it now and wonder where you are and what you are doing. Do you get enough sleep and enough to eat? Sometimes I feel sorry for your mother. It would be awful to have a child somewhere in danger and not know if they're okay.

I've been reading a lot lately, usually late at night when our little one decides to march across my belly. It's hard to see by the old oil lamp but worth it when I read the words of Emily Dickinson or Mark Twain. Did you ever read *The Good Earth* by Pearl Buck. I find books fascinating. What kind of person can just start writing a story and make it interesting enough that someone wants to read it? I read a lot, mostly on Sunday afternoons. Sometimes I fall asleep. Thank goodness we have a day of rest except for feeding the livestock.

Sometimes I sew, too. I have four dresses that need to

be finished now. For each one, I try to do something special so it will not be like anyone else's.

Papa tells me he is considering marrying that ol' Ellie Parsons. I've gotten to know her a lot better, and she's not so bad after all. I guess I was just too raw after Momma died.

The boys are doing well and still want me to come home and live. I really should have stayed there when we got married, but it is all water under the bridge now.

The early tomatoes are getting ripe real fast. The late ones will be right behind them. It's the same with the early cucumbers.

Doris and I canned fifty-six quarts of tomatoes and forty quarts of tomato juice this week. If I never see another tomato, it will be too soon. I do know they will taste good this winter. We also canned twenty-nine quarts of pickles. There will be another picking tomorrow.

There was a man that came through here last week taking family pictures. Doris and Cleve had some made, and so did I. I will send you one to keep in your hat. Of course, I'm a little bigger now than I was when you left. I can't believe I weigh 118 pounds. I weighed myself on Mr. Dawson's scales at the feed store.

I wonder what Momma would have thought about being a grandmother. There are so many things I would like to talk to her about. Why is it that we never ask the right questions when we have our important people with us? And why is it we never learn?

Just two-and-one-half months, and our little one will be here. I know there's not much chance, but I do wish you could come home. Your mother and I got the layette finished, and the clothes and quilts are beautiful. We made four dozen diapers. I hope that is enough. There are four little dresses and six gowns with drawstrings around the bottom. They are plenty long for lots of legroom. Ella Pinson said we could use her bassinet for a few months.

Your Dad has been in the barn a lot lately, and when I went to check on him last Tuesday, he would not let me come in. On Friday he gave me a dresser that he had made especially for the baby. It's beautiful. It has four large drawers. He put it up in our room. It's pretty crowded there now, but I don't mind.

It rained very hard Saturday evening. After it quit, I went out to the barn to see Biscuit. I was walking along the edge of the creek when the ground gave way, and I slid on my behind right down into the creek. I sat there for a few seconds to get my bearings. When I looked around, there was a big bobcat at the top of the bank looking at me. I screamed, and it took off. When I made it to the top of the creek bank, Cleve was standing there with a shotgun. He was so pale. He thought I had hurt myself. I told him only my pride was damaged. At supper that night, we were able to laugh about it.

Loretta came over one day last week. She said she heard some ladies at the general store talking about me and what pretty clothes I made. They were checking out the one I had left there. Maybe I will get some more business. Maybe I will open my own dress shop. Maybe I will quit rambling and go to bed. I miss you. Write soon. Tell me at least what country you are in if you can.

Evan, I really do love you. Come home soon.

Love and prayers,
Neaaka

August 2, 1942

*D*ear Evan,
It has been so hot here. Wherever you are, I don't know if you are too hot or too cold, if you are hungry or lonely. Evan, I am so worried.

The crops are in, and most have been canned and put away except for the late stuff.

I'm still saving what I make sewing and my allotment. I tried to give your mom and dad some money, and they said no. I have four dresses to make by the first of September. They are going to be beautiful, at least in my eyes.

I have two months left before our little one gets here. I can't wait. I worry sometimes that my skin will just give out and break. Do you think that's possible? Evan, there is so much I don't know. I try to learn everything I can, but I get overwhelmed. If my skin stretches do you think my brain will stretch also?

I have dreams, Evan, of being more than just a housewife and mother. I want to travel and see the world. I know you think I'm a dreamer, and maybe I am, but that doesn't mean it couldn't happen.

Biscuit had a cut on his leg last week. I'm not sure how he got it, but I made a poultice from peach tree leaves and put it on there for three days. When I took it off, the infection was gone, and it showed signs of healing. He's doing fine now. Your Dad said he never heard of such a thing. Anyway it worked.

Evan, I am getting so big, I feel like I waddle when I walk.

Your Uncle Wilbert stopped by on Wednesday and was making quacking noises while I was cleaning out the hen house. Somehow a shovel full of hen poop just popped out of the shovel and went all over his shoes. Did you know he talks dirty sometimes? I don't like him.

I found a book in the library a couple of weeks ago about Indians. It is awful how they were treated. The kids at school sure had their nerve saying things to me. If they would try it now, I would not be timid and let them get away with it. That ol' Charles Pearson had better stay out of my way. He was the worst bully in school except Wes Hansen. I'm rambling again, Evan. I do that from time to time. It's like thinking out loud. I get myself in trouble sometimes. I never know when to just shut up.

This is going to be a short letter; I have to work on the dresses before bed. I may get one of them finished. I think I need a camera so I can take pictures of the clothes I make. I saw something at the library called a portfolio. That is where you keep a record of all your work, and if you ever want a big job, you show them your portfolio. Right now I draw my designs and keep the drawings. If I had a camera, I could show the finished product on a model, the model being the person I made it for.

Will close for now, sweetheart, and will write again in a few days. Tell me what you eat and how you sleep. I imagine all sorts of things. Maybe you could set my mind at ease.

Love,
Neaaka

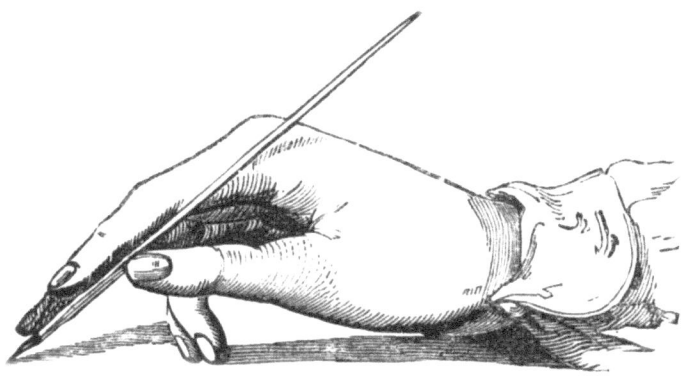

September 7, 1942

*D*ear Neaaka,

It's so good to hear from you and home. You sure ask a lot of questions, but I'm glad you are curious.

I slept in a pup-tent when we first got here. Later they put in some big tents. We didn't have beds, so I slept on the floor of the tent until they got the big tent up and the cots finally got here. You said it was hot there, and I'm sure it is, but I'm also sure it is nothing compared to here. I wonder if this place has ever seen a drop of rain. So don't worry about me being cold, although I long for that some-times. The food is not too bad. Don't worry about me. We have it pretty good right now. There's some who have it much worse. I can't tell you where I am right now. When I have things I can tell you, I will. Your letters are coming by V-mail right now. Please continue to write only on one side.

I'm glad you were able to take care of Biscuit. Why don't you like Uncle Wilbert? Reckon I will have to read your diary to find out why. I get letters from Mom, but she rarely mentions you. I always ask her about you. We use our helmets and cool water to shave. Because of the scarcity of water, we can go three days without shaving.

All of our equipment is the color of sand, to make us less visible I guess.

Neaaka, I want to know everything about home, especially little things that seem like nothing at all to you, because, trust me, there's nothing here like home or even close. I never thought I would miss the smell of fresh mown hay or the first whiff of the barn in the early morning. Sometimes at first light, I pretend I can hear the old rooster crow. There are times when I feel certain I'll see home again and then times when I fear I'll never see anything familiar again.

I know it's all in God's hands.

I hope I get to see our baby and hold him or her and teach them things like a father does, but I get to thinking sometimes that it may never happen. Keep me in your prayers. I'll never forget that even on our wedding night you got down on your knees to pray, and made me kneel beside you, and you prayed out loud. I remember that, and it gives me a warm feeling of safety. I was going to ask if you still do that, but I know that you do. That's what makes you so strong. I feel so lucky to have you for my own.

The countryside is beautiful here from what I can tell. It's just a different kind of beauty. There are no trees, just shrubs and sand. Water is scarce, so we have to be careful as I mentioned before. I hate war. It seems so senseless. I know it must be done to keep our country safe.

I am going to stop now and turn in. Five o'clock comes

early. It comes early on the farm, too, but on the farm I didn't have to wonder if I will see tomorrow or not. I reckon I'm just a little down and missing home. Just write to me often. I love you dearly and can't wait to see you and our child.

Love you and miss you,
Evan

October 3, 1942

*D*ear Evan,

I was hoping you could come home before you went overseas and into the unknown, but I guess that wasn't meant to be. There are times when I think that would be exciting. Never knowing from one day to the next what was going to happen, instead of knowing from moment to moment that every day was going to be pretty much the same. I guess there's some comfort in that but not much excitement.

Evan, I am so big. I did not know that my skin could stretch like that.

Cleve put some turnips away yesterday, and your mom and I canned mustard and turnip greens. I am so tired, but I feel like I can't complain. I'm not fighting a war.

I got Artabelle's dress done, and she loved it. Her mom and dad were a little put off because it was almost backless. Maybe in the future I will use more lace. I charged her thirty dollars, and she gave me forty. Our little savings for our farm is adding up. I help your mom and dad from time to time with getting things when they will let me.

The old Carson Farm here on six-mile is for sale. Do you remember it? It has five rooms and eighty acres. They are asking $1,400 dollars for it. It may be a year or two before I have that much, but I will keep eyes open.

I took Cleve's truck and went to see Vonnie and the baby a few days ago. Guess what? Over in Sweet Run they now have a lawman. He looks to be about Cleve's age. He stopped me and told me I was driving on the wrong side of the road. I told him the road was so narrow it only had one side. He was not impressed. He said he was going to give me a ticket.

I said, "A ticket to what?"
He just looked at me and told me to get on up the road which is what I was doing before he stopped me. I still don't know what the ticket was to.

Vonnie asked me if I wanted to change Sam. He had a dirty diaper on, but I didn't care. He is so cute. Doris and I made lots of diapers. I may get a dozen of store bought ones too.

My back has been hurting a lot. Doris says the baby

may come sooner. She said sometimes that happens, especially with the first one.

Evan, I had the radio checked out and mailed it to you on Friday. It works very well. Evan, I am so proud of you and the job you are doing.

I'm reading more and more of your mom's books. I especially like Emily Dickinson's book of poems. I know I've told you before. I wonder sometimes if I could write like that. Lots of words go through my head, but they never make it to the paper.

Your mom's brother is coming over Sunday. I don't like him. I know he's your uncle, but I still don't like him. Maybe someday I will tell you why.

We had a little frost this morning, so all the flowers are looking sickly.

I can't wait until it's just you and me and our baby in our own little home. I dream about that day. I dream about you, too. Come home soon.

Love you and miss you,
Neaaka

October 25, 1942

$\mathcal{D}$ear Evan,

Hope you are doing well. I have big news. You are the father of a beautiful baby girl. She has jet black hair and big blue eyes. She weighs around six pounds. I will take her over to the feed store in a few days and weigh her. Her name is Noralynn Mae. I named her Mae after my momma. Her name was Nyoka Mae.

Do you remember when I told your mother that having a baby couldn't hurt any worse than rolling down the hill and landing in a briar patch under a log? Well, I was wrong. It felt more like a gnat's ass being stretched over a wash tub. I'm pretty sure Noralynn will be an only child.

I didn't know something happened like a water sac breaking. It was terrible. I was walking back from the barn, and all of a sudden it felt like someone hit me in the back with a shovel. By the time I got to the front porch, I thought I had peed all over myself. You father came out the front door, and I was so embarrassed. He saw me doubled over in pain with water all over the porch. He called to your mom and said, "Doris, Neaaka's water broke." I thought that was the stupidest thing I ever heard. How do you break water?

I was looking at Noralynn yesterday. She looks so innocent and helpless. I thought how empty her brain must be, just waiting to be filled up. I heard my papa say one time that baby's brains are like sponges; they soak up everything. I decided that's an awesome responsibility. I sure hope we can fill it with the right things. I want her life to be an accomplishment and each moment to have meaning. Life is given to us like a flat piece of land, and it has to be developed. I hope when her piece of land is developed it is like a gorgeous garden for everyone to admire.

She's a very good baby. I'm teaching her to sleep in her bassinet so we won't have to break her from it later. It's very hard to not put her in the bed with me. She's so cuddly.

I will write more later, I'm so tired right now and still have two dresses to work on.

May God keep you safe and bring you home to us. That is my prayer.

Love and prayers,
Neaaka

November 11, 1942

*D*ear Evan,
        It seems like such a long time since I've heard from you. I know it hasn't been, it just seems that way. I miss you so much.

Noralyn is three weeks old now. Sometimes I call her Nora for short. Evan, she is so pretty. She's got my black hair and your blue eyes. She smiles sometimes, and it just melts my heart. I've been told she's much too young to smile, but I know a smile when I see one. I'm going to take her into town next week and have her picture made. I will send you one as soon as I get them.

I'm working on three wedding dresses, two aprons, and a church dress for Mrs. Dawson.

Noralyn just lies on the bed and looks around. I'm using the foyer outside our bedroom for sewing also. If this keeps up, I'm going to need my own shop.

I took Noralyn for a walk today and introduced her to Biscuit. She didn't seem too impressed. I'm surprised your mother doesn't pay much attention to her, but your father is a sucker for that little girl.

Do you remember that big maple tree on the hill behind the barn? Its leaves are bright red. The hills are alive with color right now. All that color behind the barn is so picturesque. I hope you can visualize it in your mind.

Mrs. Martin and her daughter stopped by this morning to look at my drawings for Gina's wedding dress. Mrs. Martin thought they were too daring for a young girl, but Gina loved them. I'll make a few changes to keep both of them happy.

A bolt came off the treadle on the sewing machine. I thought my sewing days were over. Luckily, I was able to fix it.

Evan, are you still in clerical school? I'm so glad you are not in combat. At least I hope you're not.

Uncle Wilbert came by to see the baby. I don't like that man. He and your mother were very upset that I would not let him hold Noralyn.

Evan, we hear a lot of stuff on the radio. We assume it is true. We heard that the Battle of Stalingrad began in August, and that even civilized men and boys were made to assist the Red Army in its defense. I don't know what the Battle of Stalingrad is or where it is, but it must be important to be on the news. We also heard that the RMS Laconia carrying civilians, allied soldiers and Italian POWs, was torpedoed off the coast of West Africa and sunk. Evan, I just think about all those young men and their families. My heart breaks for them. War is a terrible thing. Have you been in any battles at all? I worry about you.

We've already had a little frost, but the goldenrod is tough. It still hangs on. The creek banks are covered with it. The frost is coming soon, and the leaves on the trees will fall off fast. Do you think that's why they call this season fall? This morning the fog rose over the hill behind the barn. It looked so beautiful and mysterious. I wondered what mysteries might be hidden deep in those hollows. I was getting all poetic like I thought Emily Dickinson might be and then laughed to myself. The mysteries in those hollows are probably moonshine stills.

When Noralyn gets a little older, I would like to go into Memphis and look for some different kinds of material. I may try and order some from *Sears and Roebuck* or *National Bella Hess* catalogs.

Evan, I've been trying my hand at writing some poetry. When I write one that I think is good enough I'll send it to you. Maybe I'll draw a picture on it to scare the enemies away. Well, I have to feed Nora and put her down for a nap. I will work on my designs and maybe do some sewing.

I love you, Evan. Please stay safe.

Love,
Neaaka

December 19, 1942

*D*ear Neaaka,

I'm no longer doing clerical work. I've been sent to a very strange country. I'll try and tell you about it when I can.

War stinks! I was so sure when I got to the front, all the men would be rallying around wanting to kill the enemy. That's not the case. No one wants to be here, and it's easy to see why.

We are ready, but we don't know for what. I wonder just what it is we are fighting for. I've heard some say we must fight here; we can't allow this war to come to the shores of America. I totally agree. We hear a lot of propaganda, and the higher-ups tell us we are heroes. How can you be a hero and take a man's life? There is so much confusion in my head. We're taught that the Ten Commandments say, "Thou shalt not kill." Does war make it okay? I think not.

I'm sure our enemies are just like us with families who love them and are waiting for them to come home. The same way you are waiting for me.

Neaaka, these men do not want to be here. They want to be home with their families. These men are also committed to this war and winning to make the world a safer place. I do not want to be here, but there's no way I would leave until the job is finished.

Sometimes we talk about killing as many as possible so we can go home. I'm sure our enemies say the same thing. I know it's war, but why can't people mind their own business in their own country, and maybe there'd be no wars. Neaaka, it changes a man to see so much death and destruction.

I'm so sorry, sweetheart. I should be writing you only pleasant things, except there aren't any. I am so hot. I think in a couple of days we're going to move to some different tents and have a couple of hot meals. I'm told some of our unit will be moved to Tunisia, wherever that is, but I don't know why.

I'm trying real hard to stay alive so I can meet my little girl. Thank you for holding the home front down. I thank Mom and Dad, too.

Mom finally mentioned you in her last letter. She said you were a great seamstress and a very good mother. She said you were very independent and didn't rely on her for anything even though she was willing to help. She said you take care of your chores and your sewing all while taking care of Nora. She said Artabelle's dress was the most beautiful she had ever seen. I'm sure she wouldn't want you to know, but she's very proud of you.

Do you remember walking up Gimlet Hollow? Did you ever notice how beautiful it looks reaching for the sky? The trees are almost hidden with the gray mist, and a streak of sunshine causes it to scurry away and wait for another day. Just a random thought.

I asked for combat duty because I thought I should be more than a pencil pusher. I sure would like to be back there counting inventory. Our duty and what we really want are just not the same thing. The end result of this war, however, is the same thing.

I sent you some extra money to put toward our own place. It's only twelve dollars, but every little bit helps.

I miss you, Neaaka. It takes a little longer for mail to get to us now. The last time I received mail I got four letters all at once. I was in heaven. The package you sent with the chocolate and the homemade cookies was wonderful. I could tell you tried real hard to pack the cookies carefully, but the crumbs were good anyway.

I think sometimes about what you write in your diary. I can't wait to read it and know your thoughts.

Please excuse the sand on the paper. I never want to see sand again, so don't be planning any beach trips. Ha, ha. Next time you send a package, I could use some stationery. Keep looking for our little farm. I hope you can find something close to Mom and Dad. You know we will inherit that someday.

Remember, I told you about some of the guys having nicknames? I was talking about my coon dog and how I love to go hunting. I'm now "Coonie." I don't quite know how I feel about that. I'd rather have a manlier, fun nickname, but it makes me one of the guys. I can be "Coonie" Moore for a while.

Honey, I'll close for now. I may not be able to write as often for a while, but know I love you and can't wait to be home.

Sometimes there may be some blackouts in my letters, remember I told you that before.

Please say some prayers for me and try not to let your temper get the best of you.

Love always,
Evan

Life goes on

1943

January 6, 1943

*D*ear Evan,

I haven't heard from you for a while. I'm starting to worry a bit. Christmas was just like any other day, except we were very thankful for what little we had. We thought about you and wondered how you were spending the day.

There was no sugar for baking and no gas rations, so Biscuit got a workout.

Noralyn is so pretty and growing well. I took her over to Mr. Dawson's store and weighed her. She weighs twelve pounds and four ounces.

I saw your mother really looking very closely at Noralyn last Saturday. I think she was trying to decide how much Indian blood was in her. Your mom picked her up and held her close. She didn't know I could see her. It was a touching moment.

Noralyn has had the sniffles for a couple of days. I'm sure it's nothing. One of the ladies at the feed store told me the measles had been going around. Some people think it is better to let a baby go ahead and get the childhood diseases while they are young, and it doesn't hurt them as bad, but I don't want our baby to be sick, so I'm not taking her out anymore for a while.

Evan, it's cold here, and I wonder if you're warm enough or if you have enough rations.

Do you remember the old dead sycamore tree up on the hill behind the barn? I looked at it last night in the twilight. There was just something about it that reminded me of Jesus on the cross, except it seemed that he was vulnerable. It's hard to think of Jesus like that, but I guess he was vulnerable at that point in his life. I was standing on the back porch, and I Immediately felt the need to pray. I dropped to my knees and prayed for you. I had a sense of peace that you would come home safe and sound.

Noralyn is waking up so I will have to go.

Oh, I made three dresses and one wedding dress this past week. The wedding dress was simple, so it didn't take long.

Mr. Nettles who had the farm next to this one died last week. The farm may come up for sale soon. I will look into it. I love you, Evan. Hurry home.

Love and prayers,
Neaaka

P.S.: Evan, I think about you and how it must feel to be away from your family, and I imagine the horrors of war. So I tried to be Emily Dickinson for a few minutes. So here goes. I'm trying to write it from your point of view.

War is a thief
It steals our young men
And rages the hearts of the old
It causes nightmares before my helpless sight
Rations decide what I will eat tonight.
Bloody, weary, and tired upon my feet
Brave men and boys march on
We dream of rest as we trudge through the distant
misty fog.
Drunk with fatigue and aching bones
Though many, we travel alone.
Never tell your children the glories of war
They must never know what is in store
The weeping a grown man does
The anticipation of the sun's morning glow.

But then to see the horrors that await
Alas, who knows their fate?

Much love and prayers,
Your Wife

February 4, 1943

*D*ear Loretta,

I know it's been a while, but having a baby makes for a busy life.

I'm getting more and more orders from the general store.

It's been three weeks now since I've heard from Evan. I talked to his mom and she hasn't heard anything either. I'm sure everything is okay. I can't help but worry a little.

I read Matthew chapter six again the other day. I'm trying to live by faith, but sometimes I wobble a bit.

How are you and your banker friend doing? Is there any talk of marriage? I know I'm getting a bit nosy, so you had better write to me.

You should get Aunt Martha to bring you over so you can see Noralyn. She is a beauty. I'm not the only one who thinks so. I already want her to stay little and innocent, but that's not realistic. I know I can't protect her from life, so I will teach her the best I can. I sing "Jesus Loves Me" to her every night. She watches me and smiles. By the time she knows how to talk, she will also know how to sing this song. There's so much I want to teach her.

Are you still going to school, and what are you learning? I am so anxious to hear from you.

By the way, I wrote a poem and sent it to Evan. It dawned on me after I sent it that it should have been cheery, but I was thinking about the war when I wrote it.

Loretta, why is it that I'm sixteen years old, and I feel like an old woman? I don't know what it would be like to just lie in bed until I decided to get up. In my whole sixteen years, I've never done that. I know I've told you that before, but it's still true. Even when I was little, breakfast was at a certain time, and if you weren't up and ready, you didn't eat until the noon meal. That is one of my dreams, to sleep until I decide to get up. I guess I'm a little tired.

Looking forward to hearing from you.

Tell me all the news.

As Always,

Neaaka

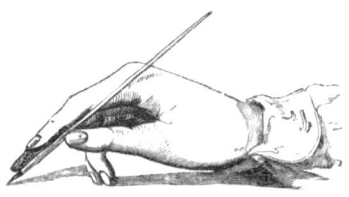

March 16, 1943

*D*ear Neaaka,

It was so good to hear from you. The bank fella, ha ha, and I are engaged. It just happened on Sunday, and I couldn't wait to tell you. He says we will have to live with his grandparents. I really don't want to do that just starting out a new marriage, but I understand he is their only support, and they are very nice. His grandfather sometimes has a sting to his voice, but I guess I can live with it.

Mr. Dawson finally heard from his son. He had been somewhere where no mail could get out. They were so relieved.

I have finished school and am working for the bank. I like it very much. My mother had a fit. She thinks it is improper for a young lady to work. I told her many women are working in factories and helping out in the war effort.

I'm sure Evan is fine; he may be somewhere like Mr. Dawson's son. I know he will write when he can.

I was at the general store last week and saw the dress you had there and some of your designs. They were beautiful. If I could afford it, I would order some, but I'm saving my money because I want you to design my wedding dress. I've heard that Artabelle's dress was the most beautiful ever, but I want you to make mine prettier. You are so talented.

I heard that Mr. Nettles died. Is Cleve going to buy his land when it goes up for sale?

Well, must close for now. Have to get ready for work. I wish we could get more rations for shoes. Mine are just about worn out, but I keep them clean and polished so they don't look so bad.

I will come over with one of your aunts to see you soon. I can't wait to see that little girl.

Sincerely,
Loretta

April 5, 1943

*D*ear Ms. Diary,
　　　I did something this week. I don't know if

it was proper or not, but I went to see Mrs. Nettles about her property. I know things like that are a man's job, but I'm just as smart as any man, and if I don't do things, how else will I learn? She is going to sell the property, and I'm going to buy it. I will buy it first and then tell Doris, Cleve and Evan. I asked Mrs. Nettles not to say anything. She's going to Memphis to live with her daughter. She's asking $2,100 for the house and eighty-five acres. I thought that was a lot, but with all the sewing and saving I've been doing I have $1,900, and she will take the rest in payments. I'm so excited I can hardly stand it.

I will get busy designing some more wedding dresses and whatever else I can do to get the savings built up.

Mrs. Nettles is leaving most of her furniture; she said there wasn't room at her daughter's. So when Evan comes home we can move into our new home, or maybe I can move in before. It's a five-room house, so Noralyn can have her own room. I feel like I'm living in a dream world. I will pay her on Thursday, and she will give me the deed.

Evan will be so excited. When I get enough money saved, I will buy a couple of cows and a bull to put in the pasture. Mrs. Nettles had already sold hers, but she is letting me keep the horse. There is a plow and some other things in the barn. I'm just sixteen and own my own farm. Yep, life is good.

Night Ms. Diary

June 6, 1943

*D*ear Ms. Diary,

I'm in shock! A big black car drove up in front of the house on Monday. Evan got out and started walking up the path to the house. He was limping and seemed to be in terrible pain. I finally gained some composure and ran to meet him. He had been wounded, and they don't need him in the war anymore. He is home, and I can't decide if I'm glad or not. He seems a little different.

The smile on his face when he saw Nora was priceless. He sat her on the sofa and walked off, so I can see he has a lot to learn.

He has been in bed mostly since he's been home or sitting on the sofa staring off in space. I guess it will take a while for things to return to normal, whatever normal will be. I really wasn't expecting him home anytime soon, so I haven't told anyone I bought the Nettles property.

I just got everything worked out with Mrs. Nettles, and she was true to her word and didn't say anything about my buying the property. The longer I wait the harder it is to tell. I was going to tell Doris and Cleve, but just haven't yet. I'm scared and I don't know why.

I asked Evan today if he wanted to go for a walk, and he about bit my head off.

He said do I look like I want to go for a walk? Have you seen what's left of my leg? What's the matter with you? So I asked if he would like to go for a ride in his dad's truck and he yelled at me, "No, damn it, I don't want to go anywhere."

Later in the afternoon, he asked me where I had wanted him to go, and he seemed a little better. I asked him to come downstairs, I had something to tell him and his parents. I was shaking so bad the words trembled as they came out of my mouth.

We were seated at the kitchen table, and I said, "I need to tell you all three something. You all know I've been working and saving to buy our own place." They all nodded their heads. I told them I had bought the Nettle's place. The surprised look on their faces was something I will never forget.

Cleve was the first to speak up, He said, "Neaaka you're just a kid. How could you buy something like that without talking it over with us first?"

Doris was in utter shock, and Evan was grinning from

ear to ear. He jumped up and hugged me so tight. He said he was so proud of me. When I told them what I had paid for it and that I still owed two hundred dollars. Cleve said, "That's a lot of money."

Evan said, "Have you met my wife? Don't you see what she has accomplished in the last year? I've been lying around upstairs ever since I came home, and she has worked on her sewing, she's cleaned house, she's been taking care of Nora, all with no help from me. Well, that's going to change." He turned and looked at me with such pride on his face and said, "Can we go look at our new home now?"

My heart is so happy. We all had been to the Nettles' home many times before, but today it was the Moores' farm.

On the way over, Evan was talking about what he was going to plant in the spring. There are a few things we can still plant this year, but spring will be a new start. He was bubbling with excitement. His mom and dad seemed excited also. They asked questions about how I could have managed this all by myself. I didn't see what the big deal was. I gave Mrs. Nettles the money and she trusted me for the rest and handed me the deed.

Evan and I will be moving into our new home after I finish the orders I have for dresses right now. They will probably be done in about two weeks. We have to apply for our own rations and get a few things stocked up. We might stay over there a night or two just to see what it's like to have our own place.

I actually felt grown up when we were looking around. I kind of liked it. I will have to write Papa and Grandpa. All's right with the world, Ms. Diary.

I'm going to find a good hiding place for you. For right now you are going to live in the bottom of my rag basket.

Till next time.

I'm going over to our farm tomorrow and find a good hiding place for you. Sorry. You will probably always have to live in the dark.

Night Ms. Diary

July 12, 1943

*D*ear Ms. Diary,

I made a great hiding place for you. I went over to our farm today while Nora was asleep. I asked Doris to keep an eye on her until I got back. There were a few tools in the barn, and I took a hacksaw with me.

There is a little pantry off the kitchen. I figured I would probably be the only one who ever used it, but just to be on the safe side, I loosened a board on the side near the front of the pantry. I put in part of a two-by-four that I had measured and cut in the barn. I brushed away all the sawdust and kicked it around in the dirt on the barn floor so no one would notice something had been cut. I put the piece of two-by-four behind the board so when I hide you there you won't fall under the floor. Then I took the hacksaw and cut off four nails. I found them in the barn also.

I nailed them into the board so it looks like it's nailed to the wall, but it really isn't. The board looked a little loose, which it was, so later in the day I went back with some honeycomb that I had chewed on to make it sticky and used it to hold the board in place. Now I can get to you and put you back, and no one will be the wiser.

Evan has told me he wants to read you, but that's never going to happen. We'll probably fight about it, but that's okay. I'm learning how to stand up for myself.

Evan seems changed a bit, but he's still sweet, and I love him. He's excited about having our own place, and that it is beside his dad's place is definitely a plus. We won't get much done this year, but next year will be great. I will have one room to use as my sewing room. I bet that I can make a hundred dresses in no time.

We will be able to buy a couple head of cattle and a bull. We'll probably need to have a tractor to cut hay. Evan will not be able to use a scythe. We will just have to see.

Ms. Diary, I have so many things going around in my head it's making me dizzy. I want to make curtains and slipcovers and braid rugs. I need more than twenty-four hours in a day.

Ms. Diary, I just looked out the window and saw Evan walking up through the yard, so guess we'll see how well your hiding place works. Here goes.

Til next time

July 18, 1943

*D*ear Loretta,

I am so excited for you and can't wait to meet your young man. When Evan and I are settled in our own place, we will invite you over for Sunday dinner.

I have such great news. Wait until you hear this. Evan came home on Wednesday. A big black car drove up, and Evan got out. I was so stunned I just stood there for a few minutes and then ran to meet him. He's been wounded in the war. His leg is a mess, part of his calf is missing, and the ligaments or whatever it is that makes it move right are damaged. He has a bad limp, and it may or may not get any better. Sometimes he seems bitter, and sometimes he's just glad to be home.

I have more big news. With the money I've saved from

sewing and my allotment, I was able to buy the Nettles' place. Evan was so excited, and we've been making all kinds of plans. Mrs. Nettles only took her personal things and left everything else. She moved in with her daughter over in Memphis. We are going to move into our new home as soon as we can get all the paperwork done about rations and so on.

Evan is so good with Nora. She just lights up when he walks into the room. She was running a little fever last night, but seemed to feel better today. I hate it when she doesn't feel well.

Evan is talking about getting a coonhound, I don't know why. Even if he killed a coon, they are no good to cook. Most men just nail their hides to the barn and dry them out. Some men sell the hides. It just seems like such a waste to kill an animal that you're not going to use for food. If he wanted a squirrel dog, I could understand that. I can put squirrel up for the winter.

I guess we should be thinking about getting a couple of pigs and a few chickens. Wow, that's a lot of mouths to feed.

Loretta, life is so good right now. The Lord has truly blessed me and our little family.

I'm making a new dress to put in the general store. You will have to go over and take a look. I've already started working on designs for your wedding dress. I assume that you will let me make it when the time comes. It will be beautiful. If you want anything special done to it or have any ideas, let me know. I'm so excited for you.

Nora is beginning to pull up and walk around things. That's pretty good for eight-months-old.

Aunt Mabel came over on Sunday. She could not believe that I had made enough money during such hard times to buy the Nettles' farm. I could not tell if she was proud or jealous.

Well, I'll close for now. I know you are going to be busy, but please keep in touch. Evan and I are going over to see Papa, Grandpa, and the boys this coming Sunday. It will be the second time they have seen Nora.

Neaaka

July 24, 1943

Dear Neaaka,

Just a quick note, Albert proposed Sunday. The wedding is going to be sometime in June of next year. I'm so excited. You will be making my wedding dress, of course.

I will write more next time.

Yours truly,
Loretta

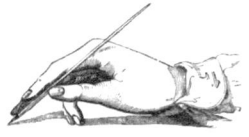

August 1943

*D*ear Ms. Diary,

I'm a little confused by what's going on now. Evan got himself an old coonhound and has started laying out in the woods half the night a couple of times a week. Then he lies around all day because he's tired. He says he just needs some time alone. I think he could be alone all he wanted working in the field cutting hay. He's been drinking a bit, also. That's something I've never known him to do. I haven't said anything to him yet, but I will eventually.

Ms. Diary, I see rough times ahead. He asked me a few days ago if he could read you. I didn't tell him no. I just asked him why he would want to read something that I felt was private. He said we are married, and nothing is private. Well, we'll see about that.

I've been working on designs for Loretta's wedding dress. They are getting married next June. I think I will tat some lace and add pearls. I lie in bed at night and think about what I can do different on each new dress, and sometimes I can dream what it will look like. Then I sketch it out. Word is getting around about my wedding dresses. I'm getting more orders than I can handle. I may have to hire someone to help, especially if Evan doesn't get on the ball.

I did get him to plow up a turnip patch on Thursday. I know how to save them for the winter, and I will can the greens.

We've lived in our little farm house about four weeks now. I'm the only one who seems to care whether all the work gets done or not, and that's getting a little old. I realize he needs some time to adjust, but I think he should be happy to be home and put everything else behind him.

Nora has come down with the measles. She is so miserable. I ground up some oatmeal and put it on her to help with the itch.

She feels real hot. I bathed her in cool water with a little alcohol in it, and it seemed to bring her temperature down some. I will probably be sitting in the rocking chair all night, but that is okay. She's ten months old now and has been walking for a month. She's pretty good to stay where I put her and tell her to stay. Last Wednesday I sat her on a blanket at the well while I was drawing water for the laundry, and she stayed there and played until I got the water drawn. She will be a great little farm girl.

I asked Evan to stay at the house with her today while I worked on Loretta's wedding dress. He said sewing, and house work, and taking care of kids is woman's work, and he will not be humiliated by doing it. I told him he didn't seem to be humiliated by not doing the man's work that there was to do around the farm. His face got so red I thought it was going to catch fire. He stood up and clenched his fist like he wanted to hit me, but I didn't back down or act scared even though I was. He finally turned and left the room and ran out toward the barn.

I started thinking about what I would do if he would ever hit me. Guess I'll have to think on that awhile. I know families are supposed to keep things private, but I think I will tell Cleve how's he's been acting. I don't think it will be much of a surprise. He's noticed a difference, but he's been making excuses for him, and so have I.

When we moved over here, he looked through all the things that were moved. I knew he was looking for you, Ms. Diary, but I knew you were safe and sound in the pantry. He hasn't asked about you anymore. I think someday he will insist. I dread that day.

Nora is worse. She sounds so congested. I covered her little chest with camphorated oil and a warm flannel cloth. It seemed to help a little. Tomorrow I will talk to Evan about taking her to the doctor.

Evan should be coming in anytime, so I'm going to put you away until another day.

Good night,
Ms. Diary

August, 1943

*D*ear Ms. Diary,

My world is gone, my life is over. I am devastated! Here I am only seventeen yet, and I've lost my momma, helped with my little brothers, stood by my husband who came back from the war wounded in body and in soul, and now I've buried my precious Noralyn, my first born. The measles along with pneumonia claimed her.

I asked Cleve to borrow his truck to take her to the doctor; he said, "Sure, go ahead." I laid her in the truck seat and started. She wasn't moving much at all, just lying there. When Evan saw me start the truck, he came running out and asked what I was doing, and so did his mother. He said he would drive.

His mother told us how stupid we were to spend two dollars on a doctor. She said that all babies have the measles and get over them just fine. I kept telling Evan we had to go, but his mother kept talking. I told him I thought Nora wasn't breathing. He punched the truck and drove as fast as he could into town to the doctor's office.

I held her and ran up the steps, praying all the way. Nora was limp in my arms. The doctor took her and laid her on the examining table. I knew, I knew she was gone. I screamed and screamed. I don't remember starting to scream or stopping. I do remember feeling numb, like this was happening to someone else.

I picked my little girl up and held her to my breast. I kind of remember Evan prying her out of my arms so they could wrap her up. I didn't want her face covered. I wanted to look at that beautiful face as long as I could. I couldn't even think about what Evan was feeling. He hadn't been home long enough to know her like I did. Why wasn't he screaming and crying? I just didn't get it.

There are many ways to suffer. I feel all of them in a firestorm of sadness. It robs my sleep, saps my strength, and changes me so much I barely recognize myself.

I do remember Papa, Grandpa and the boys coming over and staying the night. The boys tried to comfort me, bless their hearts. I love them so much.

When we brought Noralyn home from the doctor's office, Cleve looked at Evan and said, "Come on, son, we have things to do." I didn't know at the time they were going to the barn to build Noralyn a coffin. Later Cleve came and got Doris, and they left in the truck. I sat on the porch and rocked my baby. It was much later that Evan finally convinced me that I wasn't really holding her.

Doris and Cleve bought a beautiful piece of satin to line her coffin with. It was creamy white and soft. Doris even made a small pillow. Noralyn wore the pink cotton and lace dress I had made for her only three weeks before. It now seemed like a lifetime ago.

I wandered through the house in a daze. Doris was there, but I didn't want her to be. God, forgive me. I felt bitter because I knew I was blaming her for Nora's death. Maybe if she had just shut up we could have left a few minutes earlier, and the doctor could have saved her, and yet I knew it wasn't true.

Some of the neighbors came over and dug her little grave. The ceremony was simple. They talked about God and angels, and I, being a zombie, stood there speechless and motionless.

The next day when it was time to get up and milk the cow and do the day's work, I lay in bed. I never planned on getting up again. I couldn't cry any more although I wanted to. I didn't feel like I was through screaming.

Neighbors came and went, brought food, offered their condolences, and I still lay there, not talking, not caring about them, or Evan, or anyone. I wanted to go with Nora-lyn. She was all alone, and she needed her mommy.

It was five days later when I decided I had to get on with life, and I did it with a vengeance.

I stopped for nothing. When nighttime came, I wanted to be too tired to feel anything as I let blessed sleep over-take me and hoped I didn't wake up.

Tonight, dear diary, you will sleep with me. I will not let Evan find you, I promise.

October 17, 1943

ear Loretta,

It's been almost six weeks since I lost my precious Noralyn. I guess I should say we, but I feel like she was only mine. I know I'm not being fair to Evan. Maybe in time, I can do better.

Thank you for coming over with Aunt Mabel and Aunt Martha. Aunt Martha wanted to stay with me a while, and I probably should have let her, but I need to grieve on my own.

Evan is so sad. I can see it now. He's been trying hard to make things better. He is back to working more on the farm and not staying out in the woods as much.

I still have your wedding dress to do. I'm glad you like the designs. I made another design for you; I've tried to incorporate the things you liked from each design. I have three church dresses to make for the ladies in town and two more wedding dresses. I think I will hire someone to help me. I am going into Memphis in a couple of weeks to look at material for your dress. I hope to find something unusual and elegant. You will be a beautiful bride. I liked your young man very much. I know I wasn't very sociable, but I promise I will be next time.

I asked Cleve to borrow his truck to go to Memphis, then told Evan I was going. He looked at me like I was nuts and told me I couldn't go. I told him he was welcome to go with me, but one way or the other I was going. He decided he would go with me.

His limp is not as bad now, and the pain is manageable. He doesn't talk about it or complain. I guess I should try and put myself in his shoes and be more sympathetic. I'm not a very good wife. Evan's heart is broken also. I guess we should talk. I don't know what to say, so it's easier to say nothing.

I walked up the hill Saturday to visit Nora's grave. Cleve had found a stone and scratched her initials into it. I will get a headstone when I can.

I feel so old, Loretta, like I've already lived my life. There seems to be nothing to look forward to. I'm afraid Evan is going to depend on my income to keep us going, and I'm not willing to settle for that. He needs to get it together, as do I, and move on. That sounds so cold, but I've seen other people do it after a great loss. Now I know the pain inside doesn't go away; it lingers just under the surface. Sometimes it comes out in torrents of tears and sometimes unwanted tears like raindrops.

We will make it through the winter, and if Evan doesn't start to pull his weight around here, I will hire someone in the spring to do the plowing and help with the planting.

Doris hasn't been feeling very well. She mentioned that she should probably see the doctor. I couldn't help it and said, "And waste two dollars." I tasted the bitterness in my mouth. I wanted to feel bad for what I said, but I couldn't. Loretta, you must think I am a terrible person, and maybe I am. I don't know anymore.

Until next time.
Yours truly,
Neaaka

New Challenge

January 6, 1944

*D*ear Ms. Diary,

Well, Christmas has come and gone. We didn't bother going to the market to buy fruit, but I did go over to Papa's and visit.

Papa married that ol' Ellie Parsons. She seems to be a good woman, and she's good to the boys, however, they do give her a rough time. I got onto them about being so ornery. I stayed three days. Evan was glad to see me when I got home.

I went out to the barn today. I really needed to be by myself. I sat there on a bale of hay and reflected back on the past year. I tried to decide if I wished Noralyn had never been born or if I were happy that I even had her for such a short time. I decided a short time with her, even with the heartache, was so much better than no time at all. I realized how blessed I was. I recalled that little smile when I picked her up and looking at that adorable face when she was sleeping. I remembered how content she was when I read to her and when I showed her my designs. I talked to her like she understood everything I said. Who knows, maybe she did.

I sat there and talked to God. I needed forgiveness for my hateful attitude. I got mad when it came to me that I should apologize to Doris. Really? Why should I do that? But the Lord put it on my heart, so I have to do it.

Ms. Diary, I came into the kitchen on Friday, and Evan had the pantry door open looking for something. I almost had heart failure. I asked him what he was looking for, and he said, "Nothing, just looking."

I tried to act like I didn't care for him being in there. I asked him if he was looking for something to cook for me for supper. He looked at me and laughed. So maybe he didn't notice my panic. I will be keeping an eye on him and the pantry. I looked in after he went outside to see if anything was amiss. All things looked normal.

I wonder how much longer before the war will end. I've decided to be a little more upbeat and see if I feel better. Maybe I need to read some more Emily Dickinson. Maybe I should write my own poetry. Maybe I should shut up. Night, Ms. Diary.

February 9, 1944

*D*ear Loretta,

Evan and I went to Memphis on Tuesday. He wasn't real thrilled about looking at fabric, but he said he was always amazed at what I could do with it. I asked his opinion about what I chose for your dress. I think it made him feel good. It is beautiful. I hope I can sew it up without ruining it. Evan says I shouldn't worry, I always do good work. I guess I shouldn't be in a hurry though since you're not getting married until June. I have your dress cut out and will put it together in a few days. I have a lot of hand sewing to do on it, and I'm not going to get in a hurry, so sometime in March you can come over and try it on.

Evan suggested I take pictures of all the things I make, especially the things I design myself, and keep them in an album. I will have to save enough money for a camera and to get them printed. It is a great idea. I keep all my designs, but never have anything to show after it is made.

I have never been to a big city like Memphis. I wanted to walk, and walk, and walk to look at the big, tall buildings. Evan wanted to get what we came for and go home. He will not come with me again.

I apologized to Doris for my attitude with her and asked her forgiveness. She cried and asked for my forgiveness. I guess I never thought about how she felt losing her granddaughter and feeling like it may have been her fault. We both cried, and I truly forgave her. We will start over, but I don't know how long it will last.

Cleve hasn't been feeling well and has really slowed down. I'm worried about him. He is my ally. I count on him to be fair in all situations.

He told Evan to shit or get off the pot, that he has a family to take care of. He told him it was a shame that he got wounded in the war, but he should be thankful because thousands didn't get to come home. It seemed to be the pep-talk he needed. He has done much better but has begun to drink more in the evening. He said it helps dull the pain and the images in his head. I don't like it one bit. He got really drunk on Saturday night. I couldn't figure out where he got the money to buy the booze. I looked in my money jar that I use to buy fabric with, and two dollars was missing. I told him if he thought he got injured in the war, he didn't know what it was like to get hurt if he so much as looked at my jar again. He said we were married, and what was mine was his. That's how it works, he said.

I said let me tell you how it works: If you earn it, it's yours; if I earn it, it's mine. He slapped me hard across the face. I was in such shock I just stared at him. At first, I thought I would kill him, and then I thought I would wait until he goes to sleep and whip him with a switch. Then I thought I would tell his dad, but I will wait and hope it doesn't happen again, then I'll decide what I will do if it does. I do know it won't happen more than once again.

I went out to the barn later, and Evan was sitting on a bale of hay crying. He was so embarrassed that I had seen him crying. He stood up and said he was sorry and tried to hug me. However, I was not in a forgiving mood. I told him if it ever happened again, he may not live to see morning. He looked at me as though he were in shock. He said, "Neaaka, you wouldn't really hurt me would you, after all I've been through?"

I told him he wasn't the only one who had been through something bad, and that was no excuse to be less of a man and hit a woman.

He said, "You think I'm less of a man because I lost my temper and hit you? I'm sorry," he said.

I told him he could take his "sorry" and dip it in the toilet, because that's all it meant to me, and, yes, real men don't have to resort to hitting a woman to control her. Well, the story goes on and on. Loretta, are you sure you want to get married?

I'm sorry. I shouldn't be telling you all this. I will tell my diary this from here on out. I'm sure Albert will be good to you. Evan will be all right, *too,* as soon as he figures out I'm uncontrollable. It may take him awhile.

I found some little pearls in Memphis; I think I will use them on your dress. If you don't like them, I will take them off.

Next month we should start tilling the soil. I may have to plow Evan first. This year will be our first crop on our own farm. I am so excited about that and so scared that Evan may ruin it.

Tell Albert "Hi" from me. Hope to hear from you soon.

Sincerely,

Neaaka

March 1944

*D*ear Ms. Diary,

It's near the end of March, and no plowing has been done. Cleve has all his fields plowed and has been onto Evan to get busy. Evan just drinks and lies out in the woods. I'm trying to be a good wife and encourage him. I tell him all the time it will get better with time, but losing Nora doesn't get any better for me, so maybe his demons can't get better either.

Farming is not something you can put off until you get around to it. If by the first of April, he has not plowed at least the garden spot, I will hire someone. I've already told Mr. Dawson over at the feed store I was looking for help. I told Evan, too. He got so mad, he said he would do his own work and didn't need anyone's help. Well, that remains to be seen.

I made a new dress and took it over to the general store. I already have five new orders. I have to make each one different, so it's a challenge to come up with new designs on the same type of dress. I am convinced I can do anything I want if I'm willing to work hard enough. I just wish Evan could see a future. If I try to talk to him, he thinks I'm nagging. Maybe I am. I don't know.

I went out yesterday and was working on the fence. Ethel, our cow, got out and went visiting over to Cleve and Doris's. Evan came out and saw me working on the fence and got upset.

He said what if some of the neighbor's saw me? What would they think of him? I told him they would think he was a drunken S.O.B., and they would be right. At first he seemed to be real mad, and then he started laughing. He said one of the things he loved about me was that I always told the truth, and that was the truth, and he was going to do something about it. He got tools and started working on the fence. When he finished, he stood back and looked at it and said that it felt real good. Then he went to the barn, put the harness on the horse and plowed the garden and used the drag to break up the clumps of dirt. He even finished the furrows.

So tomorrow, I can start planting the garden. I burned a lettuce bed the first of March and started some plants from seed in the spare bedroom. I'm ready.

Evan was rather pleasant this evening. After supper we talked a bit. I found out about some of his dreams. He said he never wanted to be a farmer. He said with his clerical experience he would rather work in a bank or run his own business. Let me tell you, Ms. Diary, I was quite shocked. I told him if that's what he wanted to do, he should do it. And I meant it. We could hire somebody to work the farm. I could continue sewing and working on the crops. He seemed to be in such a good mood he didn't drink anything at all.

His Uncle Wilbert came by and brought him a pint of moonshine. They were sitting on the front porch laughing and talking. I saw Evan take the lid off the moonshine. I walked by and knocked the jar out of his hands and broke it. I looked at Wilbert and told him I didn't like him.

Evan laughed and said," Neaaka, don't mince words. Tell him how you really feel." He told his Uncle Wilbert not to bring anymore moonshine, he was through drinking. I felt like shouting.

After Uncle Wilbert left, Evan asked me why I didn't like him. I said it was because he was a creep. He knew there was more to it than that. I didn't really want to tell him, but I did. I told him about him grabbing my breast and the incident about hanging my underwear on the line. He was furious. He got up and said he was going to his house and knock some sense into him. I told him it was too late, he would never have any sense. I begged him to wait a few days and think things over and let his temper cool down. He said he would.

I miss my baby girl. There's a hole in my heart that will never be filled. I walk up to her grave occasionally and talk to her. She would be starting to talk a little now. Sometimes I think I can't bear the pain another day.

Well, Ms. Diary, I wonder what tomorrow holds. Tomorrow I will rise with the sun and plant my garden and be happy. I will, I will.

Later Ms. Diary,
Neaaka

April, 1944

*D*ear Ms. Diary,

Evan got the fields plowed, and we have planted for two days now. He seems to be doing well. We've laughed and worked together. It's been really nice. We'll see how it goes when it's time to hoe the corn and the garden. We've planted so much. I tried to tell him we should plant things a couple of weeks apart so they didn't come in all at once. I may not be able to work them up and get all the canning done if they do. He said, "You'll manage." He didn't say we will manage. I'm going to plan ahead and see if some neighbors want to buy any extra that we have.

Evan went into town last week and talked to Mr. Nelson about a job at the bank. Mr. Nelson said he could use the help, but couldn't pay much. Loretta's boyfriend works there, so maybe they will become good friends. He starts next Monday. He seems so much happier. I'm not sure I can keep everything together here on my own, especially since I just learned I'm going to have another baby.

Ms. Diary, at first I was so happy, and then I got really scared. Now I don't know what to feel. I don't know if Evan will help me in the evening or will say he's already put his day in. On the farm there is no end to the day until it gets dark.

Ms. Diary, I don't want to talk any more today, I'm too tired.

Neaaka

May 17, 1944

*D*ear Ms. Diary,

     I turned eighteen today, and I feel like I'm much older. Was there ever a time when I didn't have to work? I can't remember. It seems as though responsibility always rode my back like an old mare.

Ms. Diary, the most extraordinary thing has happened. It's not a good thing either, so I can't figure out why I'm so happy. I had told Mr. Dawson I might need some help here, and I do especially since Evan went to work at the bank.

I looked out the window Wednesday and saw a man walking up through the yard. I'm not sure what happened, but just seeing him made me have a funny kind of feeling. I can't describe it. It was like there was a fire in my belly. I felt sweaty and tongue tied. When he knocked on the door, it took me a few seconds to gain some composure and open the door. We stood there for what seemed like an hour just looking at each other and not saying a word. He drank me in like a thirsty man gulps water, and I did the same. Finally he said, "Hi, my name is Fred Dawson; my uncle said you may need some help here."

I stammered, "Yes, come on in." Never in my whole life had I been so nervous and tongue tied. I finally introduced myself and told him what he might be needed for and what I could pay. I figured some of the pay would have to come from my sewing.

Ms. Diary, he had a head full of curly dark brown hair with a curl dipping down onto his brow. He had a cigarette that seemed to be stuck to his upper lip. It stayed there while he talked. He never took his eyes off me nor I him. He must have been at least six feet tall and very muscular. It came to me later that the feelings I was having should have been reserved for my husband, but I have never felt like that about him. I could smell trouble in the air, and I didn't want to. I knew I should have told him we didn't need any help, but we did. I asked him to come back on Monday to start work.

Ms. Diary, I told Evan I had hired somebody to work, and he told me I didn't need anyone. I ignored him and explained that Fred Dawson would be here on Monday.

When Monday came, Evan said he didn't feel well, and he was going to stay home. I said, "No, you are not. You have a responsibility to Mr. Nelson. You can't have it both ways. Either you are going to farm, or you are going to work at the bank." Finally, he left for work.

When Mr. Dawson arrived, I was less nervous than before. I showed him around and told him what needed to be done that day. I was almost hateful with him. He tried to be nice, but the feelings he stirred in me were so new I didn't know how to handle it. He asked about my husband. I told him about the war and his job at the bank.

He said he felt funny working for a woman. I looked at

him, and I know the anger showed on my face. I told him where the door was. He said, "No, please, I really need this job." For half a second I felt sorry for him.

He went to the barn and got the horse harnessed and went to work on the back nine. I was glad he was out of sight. I couldn't figure what I so mad about. It dawned on me later I didn't want to feel what I was feeling. Lord have mercy on me. I need it desperately.

When dinner time came, I rang the bell, and he came to eat. That was part of our bargain: I would fix his dinner and supper as part of his pay. That meant he would be eating with Evan and me. I didn't bother to tell Evan this because he would have told me no. I don't take the answer "no" very well. Evan still has to learn that. I put Fred's meal on the table and told him I had things to do; I wanted so badly to sit there with him and drink him in. Instead, I went outside to work on the laundry. These feelings were so strange to me. I didn't want to have them. I wondered if he was having them, too. I knew he was by the way he was looking at me.

I was hanging clothes on the line when Fred came out of the kitchen. He walked right over to me and told me it seemed like I didn't like him, and if that was the case, he would bring his dinner and go to his uncle's for supper. That way, I wouldn't have to see him as much. I stood there with my mouth open. I wanted to see him. I wanted to see him more than anything. That was the problem, and I almost told him so. I composed myself and said, "Come on, let's go sit on the porch for a minute."

I let him know that I needed him there, and I couldn't do the plowing because I was going to have a baby, but I had not told my husband yet.

What was I thinking? He told me about his wife and how she was a little difficult to understand when she was expecting. Oh, my goodness, it never occurred to me that he might have a family. Instead he told me she had died in childbirth, and so had the baby. I then told him about Noralyn, and we commiserated about our losses. He asked me to call him Fred, and I asked him to call me Neaaka. When he went back to the field, I didn't want him to go. I wanted him to stay and talk with me. What's happening? I don't understand, Ms. Diary. Talk to you soon.

June 20, 1944

*D*ear Ms. Diary,

It's June, and all the crops are planted. Fred is working out very well. He is a hard worker and prides himself on doing a good job. He and Evan get along great. I make myself scarce when he is around.

Evan was happy when I told him about the baby. It will

be due the sixth of December. The crops will all be put up by then, and I will be sewing like a mad woman. I know another baby can never replace Nora, but I am looking forward to this child.

It's been a while since I've written to Loretta. She is getting married this month. She came on Saturday and picked up her wedding dress. It was beautiful if I do say so myself. She was very pleased. Her mother's jaw dropped when she saw it. She said it was the most beautiful dress she had ever seen, much prettier than Artabelle's. I had learned to tat lace when I was a little girl, and I made lace for the whole back and sewed pearls, not real ones of course, all through the back and across the front.

I had the dress laid out on the bed one day when I was almost through with it. Evan came in and saw it. He looked at it with awe. He said, "You did all this?" He kept looking at it and told me he could see why people wanted to buy my clothes. He told me I was talented and acted like he was proud of me. He hugged me, and it felt like he really meant it. It was good to not think of Fred. I'm trying so hard to think of Fred only as a hired hand, but it's becoming increasingly difficult. I suppress my feelings and pretend they don't exist. I try to focus on Evan and the baby I'm carrying.

I have enough money saved from my sewing to buy a truck. We really need one here. Evan would probably want to drive it to work if we had one. I have orders for six dresses from the general store. I work on them at night as much as I can. It's hard to see with the oil lamps. Doris and Cleve had electricity put in their house. I may have that done here.

Vonnie came over on Tuesday and brought her little boy. I tried not to think of Noralyn and all the cute things she would be doing. Vonnie could tell it bothered me even though I didn't want it to. It was good to see her. I didn't tell her about the feelings I was having for Fred. Ms. Diary, you are the only one I tell about that.

Vonnie asked me to make her a sundress for a picnic they are going to have at her church. It's only a couple of weeks away. I told her to go buy the material, and I wouldn't charge her anything for making it. She seemed real excited.

Sometimes I think I would like to have a big Sunday dinner and invite all of mine and Evan's family over, but then, that would mean Uncle Wilbert would have to come, and I don't want him anywhere around.

Kalinda is working in a factory over in Middleton. She has her own place with a couple of friends. Sometimes I think that is what I would like, but then I think of Noralyn and the new baby, and I wouldn't change a thing except for these feelings I have for Fred. "Please go away."

Maybe I will borrow Cleve's truck and go visit Papa, and Grandpa, and the boys. They are growing up so fast. I feel like I hardly know them. Good night, Ms. Diary.

July 12, 1944

*D*ear Loretta,
        I know it's been a while since I've written. I just have to tell you, you were the most beautiful bride I have ever seen. Everyone was raving about your dress. I have got two more orders for dresses just like yours, but I have to charge a lot more. I hate to do that, but with the crops coming in and everybody wanting to get married within a few months, I'm going to be up all night trying to get them done. Don't worry, I won't make them just like yours, but similar if that's all right with you.

How do you like married life? I really hope you and Albert are very happy. Albert seems like a great guy.

Evan has started hunting again on the weekends instead of working here on the farm. I think I won't let him eat anything I have canned if he doesn't help me. He can go find it in the woods. He never brings anything home. I suspect he's not hunting even though he takes his gun and the dog and heads into the woods. Last weekend he was gone two days. When he came home, he was all dirty, but it looked like he had rubbed stuff on him to make himself look dirty. You know, the sad part is I don't care. I tried to. I tried to act all mad and told him what I thought, but I didn't really care, except for needing help around here. I was glad he was gone.

Cleve came over on Saturday and asked where Evan was. I started to tell him he was working out in one of the fields, and then decided I would not cover for him. I told Cleve about him drinking and hitting me, about him lying out in the woods all weekend, and about not helping around here. He already knew I had hired Fred to work. He was steaming when he left. I apologized for upsetting him. He said when Evan comes home, to tell him to come over, he wanted to see him. I will gladly do that. Maybe he will take a switch to him and beat some sense into him. I told Cleve we were going to have another baby. He smiled and said he hoped that was a good thing. So do I.

The tomatoes are starting to get ripe, so I'm washing jars and getting ready to put them away. I'm so tired I can't think most of the time. I picked four pecks yesterday. That's a bushel, but I put them in peck baskets so I can carry them, and they won't get squashed.

Before Mr. Nettles died, he made a place to boil water outside. We have a gas well on our property, and it is free to us. I can carry a washtub full of water, bucket by bucket, and get it boiling, then drop the tomatoes in it and immediately take them out. The skin slides right off. I canned fourteen quarts yesterday. I will pick more today.

Last Thursday I picked two bushels of green beans. I sat on the back porch in the morning and worked on the beans. Fred, our hired hand, came in for dinner and sat down and helped me for about two hours. When the sun came in on the porch, we moved everything to the front porch in the shade. It was so nice to have help. Fred said he would help me with whatever I needed. It feels good to have help.

Loretta, I would love for you to come for a visit. I promise not to make you work. I just need someone to talk to. I have some things to tell you that I refuse to write down except in my diary.

I never mention my diary to Evan, so he has stopped asking about it. Sometimes I see him just looking through things. I know what he's doing, but I act ignorant.

My baby is due the sixth of December. I guess I should say our baby, but no, it's just mine. I'm glad it's going to be in the winter so all the work will be done, and I can concentrate on my sewing. I got Noralyn's layette out and looked at it a few days ago. My heart broke all over again. I guess I will make myself use it again. I'm beginning to show a little but not enough to wear the clothes I made when I was expecting Nora.

Loretta, I'm rambling, so I'm going to shut up. Hope to see or hear from you soon.

Neaaka

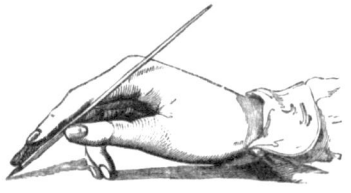

July 15, 1944

*D*ear Ms. Diary,

I am in so much trouble. I told Cleve how Evan was acting, and he gave him what for. Then Evan got mad at me and got drunk. That was not a smart thing to do. I could see him building up to something. I left the house and went out to pick beans. I asked him to go help me, and he just stared at me and said maybe I should get Fred to help.

I said, "Yes, maybe I should."

I picked a bushel and dragged them back to the house. I sat down on the front porch to string the beans, and he came out. I thought for a minute he was going to help me, but all he wanted to do was argue. I said nothing, which upset him even more. He got right up in my face and started yelling. I still ignored him. He finally hit me so hard it knocked me off my chair. He looked surprised at what he had done. He went back in the house. I got up and continued to string beans while I decided on my next course of action.

I waited about an hour and went inside. He was passed out on the floor. I got him under the arms and dragged him to the bedroom. It took some doing, but I finally got him on the bed. I went out to the barn and got some rope off the harness and found some more in a box. I went back in and removed Evan's pants and turned him on his stomach. I tied Evan's hands to the head of the bed and his feet to the foot. Then I went outside and cut two branches and went inside and wore him out. I actually drew blood.

Then I couldn't decide what to do with him. If I left him there to wake up, he might kill me when he did get up. I thought maybe I could drag him out to the barn and let him wonder what happened. He had stripes all over his body. He was going to hurt so bad when he woke up. He moaned and groaned while I was beating him. I was glad it was going to hurt.

I decided to go tell Cleve what had happened. At first he just looked at me in disbelief. Then he just grinned. He said, "Neaaka, you beat all."

He came back to the house with me and saw that I had taken Evan's pants off before I whipped him. He gasped when he saw him. We decided that we would put the harness rope and the switches and everything back in place and put him on the back porch. We were just going to let him wonder what had happened.

I had to take the quilt and wash the blood spots from it and make the bed again. Cleve went back home and tried to get me to go with him. I refused. I hoped Evan would wake up before bed time. I was so tired, but I was afraid to go to bed. Oh yeah, we put Evan's pants back on him. I finished stringing the beans and carried water to put over them until morning.

Ms. Diary, we will see what happens tomorrow.

July, 1944

*D*ear Ms. Diary,
Well, today has been interesting to say the least. I slept last night in the upstairs bedroom, hoping Evan didn't come looking for me. He didn't. When I came downstairs this morning, he was sitting on the front porch. I said, "Good morning, would you like some coffee?" He just looked at me like he couldn't figure out who I was and nodded his head yes. I brought his coffee and started back inside. He asked where I was all night. I told him upstairs. He acted relieved. He said, "I thought you left me."

I told him if he didn't get it together that's exactly what was going to happen, except I wouldn't be the one to leave. I would sell the farm, and he could go home to Mommy. He told me I couldn't do that, then immediately said he was sorry. He said I was the only person he knew who could do anything they set their mind to. I told him not to forget it.

He asked me about Fred and how I felt about him. I said, "He helps me. I like that. I look forward to his coming because I know the work will get done."

He cried. I guess all drunks cry. I really didn't care that he cried. He said he would do better. He promised. He asked me what happened to him last night. He said he looked like someone had beaten him with a switch. I told him he hit me and knocked me out of my chair, and that's what I knew about last night. The rest was on him. He asked if we had any salve because he needed to put some on.

I saw Cleve walking up through the yard. He acted like he knew nothing and said good morning. I got him a cup of coffee, and we sat on the front porch. He asked Evan what he was going to do today. He said I guess I'm going to help Neaaka pick the rest of the beans and string them. Cleve said that was wonderful, and that she could use the help. He told Evan how hard I worked at the farm, and sewing, and that I needed help.

Evan told Cleve he hurt all over and looked like he had been beat with a switch. Cleve said, "Son, what did you get into?"

Evan had to admit he didn't know but decided to give

up drinking. Cleve told him when he went hunting, it would be best if he brought something home. Maybe he should give up hunting, too. He said he enjoyed hunting, but he would think about it.

The rest of the day Evan couldn't do enough to help me. If I had known that's what it took I would have beaten his ass a long time ago.

Fred came and asked what we needed done today. Evan said he could help us pick beans and string them. The work went by quickly, and I had time to sew last night. It was a great day.

August 14, 1944

*D*ear Ms. Diary,

The war still drags on. Evan doesn't listen to the radio anymore and never talks about anything that happened to him during the war. Sometimes I feel sorry for him, and sometimes I just want to smack him. I look back to the fourteen-year-old girl who couldn't get enough of him to the eighteen-year-old who wishes he would go away and wonder what was I thinking. Of course, I know now that fourteen-year-olds don't think. They feel.

Mr. Dawson's son came home for a visit. He had an

injury from the war, but it wasn't life-threatening and didn't keep him from going back. He is Fred's first cousin, so he was happy to see him.

Ms. Diary, the fire in my loin still rages. I don't know what to do. I'm almost mean to Fred because I don't want him to suspect how I feel. I'm afraid if I look him in the eye or get close to him I will just jump into his arms and never let go. When he came on Tuesday, he asked what he had done to upset me. I told him nothing. I was with child, and things were a little crazy for me. He seemed to understand. I know I will have to make an effort not to be so contrary with him. I couldn't stand it if he quit working for me. I've made five church dresses this week and worked on a wedding dress that needs to be finished next week. No time to breathe.

Good day,
Ms. Diary

August 21, 1944

*D*ear Ms. Diary,
I've gone and done it now. Oh, my goodness. Fred worked late Friday night, and I thought he had

already left. I heard a noise out at the barn, and the chickens were carrying on. I grabbed the gun and ran to the barn and ran smack dab into Fred. I dropped the gun, and he held me close and kissed me with a passion that I had never felt. I couldn't think about right or wrong. We held each other and kissed for the longest time before I came to my senses. I didn't know what to say or do. When I tried to talk, he shushed me and held me close. I never wanted this to stop.

He finally asked me where I was going with a shotgun so fast. I was going to protect my chickens I told him. He laughed. It was the sweetest sound.

He told me about the first day he saw me and how he felt and how hard he had to fight it. He told me about how excited he was to come to work every day and know that he was going to see me for a few minutes at least. I had no idea he was feeling the same way as me. Well, I kind of did that first day, but wasn't sure.

Oh my goodness, I can get into more trouble just staying here and minding my own business. Ms. Diary, if I didn't have you to talk to, I would explode.

Aunt Martha sent word she was coming over on Wednesday. It will be good to see her. I hope Fred isn't around; she'll be able to tell things are not as they should be. I haven't told her there is a baby on the way. I am excited for her to see the dress I'm working on. She said Loretta's dress was the prettiest one she had ever seen. I love Aunt Martha.

Ms. Diary, there is a man who comes into the general store who has a truck he wants to sell. I think I will buy it.

I need to be able to go to Vonnie's when I want to, and into town. I'm sure Cleve gets tired of my borrowing his truck all the time. I could also go visit Papa and the boys. I could run away when my feelings for Fred overtake me. That's the real reason.

Evan and I hardly talk anymore, and that's okay with me, but it really shouldn't be. He is a little more helpful and does not drink. Doris is wondering what I've done to her wonderful son. I think it's not me; it's all the terrible things he saw in the war that he can't get off his mind, and he doesn't know how to cope.

I find myself looking out to see if I can catch a glimpse of Fred working. If I do, I want to run to his arms, but I mostly avoid him, and he avoids me. That's not what I want to do, Ms. Diary. I'm such a terrible person, I don't know what to do. Evan still looks for you occasionally, but never asks if I still write to you. I make sure I write to you while he is at work, and I always sit by the window so I can see if he should come home early. We girls can't be too careful.

Later

October 19, 1944

*D*ear Ms. Diary,

I'm so sad. The crops are laid up, and I don't see Fred much anymore. Sometimes he comes by just to hold me. I can't stand being away from him. I have such mixed feelings. I know it's wrong, but I'm pretty sure I love him. But I thought I loved Evan, too. How can I be sure about anything?

As much as I want my baby, I kind of wish I wasn't expecting one right now. Fred is going to work at the saw mill through the winter. He said he had thought about going to Memphis to work, but with jobs being scarce and me being here, he didn't want to leave. Goodness knows I don't want him to go.

I spend all my time sewing. One of the pillars of our community, has decided she wants me to design some children's clothing for her son and daughter. They are three and five years old. That will be fun. She wants their things to be different from anyone else's. I've made some designs, and she is coming over Tuesday to look at them. I hope she's not too hard to please.

It's so nice to have a gas stove and not have to cut wood in the winter except for the fireplace. Evan didn't bother getting wood in for the winter, but Fred saw to it that we had plenty.

Ms. Diary, we will talk another day.

November 5, 1944

*D*ear Ms. Diary,

This time next month my baby should be here. I'm both excited and a little fearful. It will be wonderful to hold my baby in my arms, but I know I will always wonder what Noralyn would have been like and what she would have looked like.

I've been having some cramps lately, and I worry about the baby. I just trust that everything will be all right. Evan has been coming home and going hunting after work.

Why would anyone want to go out in the cold and stay in the woods? He takes both dogs and doesn't come in until very late. I don't understand it. He rarely ever talks to me, however, he is always ready to eat the meal I put on the table. I think tomorrow I won't fix anything and see what he has to say about that.

My back hurts so badly, and he does not offer to help with the feeding of the livestock at night. I think I may have to ask Cleve or Fred for help.

This is certainly not my idea of what marriage was going to be like. Sometimes I think I don't like him much anymore. I will try harder since we do have a baby coming. Sometimes I remember when I was a stupid little girl writing him letters, and I realize my Momma was right: fourteen was too young to know your own mind. I'm eighteen and feel like I've already lived my life. There must be more out there. I long for something; I just wish I knew what it was.

I'm worried about Cleve. He has slowed down so much. He's my buddy. I think if anything happened to him, I wouldn't want to live here anymore. Doris seems a little easier to get along with now. I don't know what the change is, but it is for the better.

I hope how soon the war ends. What if it doesn't end? What if it just goes on and on? It was difficult last summer to get canning jars. I'm grateful Mrs. Nettles left hers here.

I seem to be looking backward instead of forward. I need to change my attitude. Ms. Diary, sometimes I'm glad you don't talk back, though sometimes I wish you did. Maybe it wouldn't be so lonely.

Evan is off work tomorrow, and I think I may try to talk with him at least to clear the air. Who knows? It might do some good.

Fred is staying away all the time now. I hear nothing from him.

Ms. Diary, I've felt sorry for myself long enough. It's time to get on with the business at hand. I have four dresses, two shirts, some children's clothes, and a new wedding dress to sew. I won't be doing much sewing next month when the baby gets here. I guess I should be thinking about names. The only thing I'm sure of is if it's a boy, I will not be calling him Evan.

Time to put you up and get busy. Tomorrow is another day.

Good night,
Ms. Diary

November 13, 1944

ear Ms. Diary,
I've just about quit writing Loretta. I'm afraid she will think I'm a terrible person because of Fred. I am so confused. I want my life here on the farm with my

husband, but I want him to be who he was before the war. I think that's not going to happen. I think about Fred and see a whole different life, like maybe a little dress shop where I design all my own clothes and make extravagant dresses for the rich ladies, not that there are many of them around anymore.

Vonnie is expecting another baby. Little Sammy is almost two years old. I think about my Nora so much. She would be nineteen months old now.

Aunt Mabel came over on Sunday, and we had Sunday dinner. I know she could tell that things weren't right with Evan and me, but she didn't say anything. She just looked at me with sad eyes.

I'm so tired. Ms. Diary, sometimes I think I can't take another step, or wash another load of clothes, or do anything else. I want to lie down and stay there until I get ready to get up.

Be a good girl, Diary. We will talk tomorrow.

November, 1944

*D*ear Ms. Diary,

I hate, hate, hate, Evan Moore. I want to kill him. Ms. Diary, you will too when you find out what he did. Evan came in yesterday, and I was in so much pain. I knew my baby was coming early and asked Evan to go get help. He said he was going hunting. I asked him to please go get Ms. Winters, the midwife, or at least go get his mother. He left for a minute and came back with a rope and tied my hands and feet to the bed. I screamed at him to please get Ms. Winters. He said, "You think I didn't see the marks on my wrist and ankles when you tied me up and beat the shit out of me with a switch? I don't know how you managed it, but I know you did."

He was drunk again and just laughed. He said this wasn't his baby. It was Fred's. I tried to tell him I didn't even know Fred when I got with child. I had never been with anyone else. He didn't believe me. He left me all alone. I lay there for what seemed like hours.

My little baby was born with no one to hold him or her and never took his or her first breath. I screamed and screamed in agony, but no one heard.

Evan came in long after it got dark. He lit the lamp and looked at me. I begged him to please untie me and let me hold my baby. He picked my baby up by the arm, and put it in a little box, and left with it, and came home without it. I asked if it was a boy or girl. He said, "Neither, it was a bastard."

I asked what he did with it. He told me to forget it; he would never tell where it was.

I am so numb. I need to go home and see Papa and Grandpa. My heart is so broken. I don't know if I had a son or a daughter. God, help me. I'm going to leave Evan, and if I never see him again it will be too soon. He did untie my hands, but not my feet. When I gained enough strength, I was able to untie them, but it took me over an hour. By then, I was too weak to get up.

I've got a little money saved from my sewing. I may go to Memphis and set up a dress shop or do something to get away from here. I will talk to Cleve when I am able to go over there. I don't know who this man is, who I thought I loved. I can't think anymore tonight. I have to have a plan together by morning. I will sleep upstairs tonight with a shotgun in the bed with me. I pray to God that I don't have to use it.

Good night, Ms. Diary

November, 1944

*D*ear Ms. Diary,

I wasn't able to get up the stairs last night. I was able to get the shotgun and put it in bed with me. I was so weak all I could do was lie there and hope he didn't come back and prayed that I was having a nightmare, and when I woke up everything would be all right.

I had to lie there in all the mess and blood. I couldn't carry any water to clean up with. I prayed for Cleve to come over and for Evan to stay gone, but neither happened.

I could hear Evan in the kitchen. I thought maybe he was getting a knife or something to finish me off. At this point I didn't care. My whole life was a nightmare. I fell asleep sometime in the night and didn't wake until early afternoon the next day.

I could hear Evan talking to someone, and then I realized it was Cleve. I wanted to scream for him to help me, but I couldn't. Cleve never came in. I heard Evan tell him I was upstairs sewing. This was his son, and he would be devastated. I made up my mind right then I would never tell anyone what had happened to me. I figured no one would believe me anyway. In my wildest imagination, I could never believe that one human being could do that to another.

I had to plan on how I was going to explain that there was no baby. I would just say it was stillborn and was buried up on the hill with Noralyn. I really hoped it was. Sometime in the afternoon Evan came into the room and looked at me in horror and asked what had happened to me. I told him he happened, and he acted like he was in shock. I asked him what he did with my baby. He began to cry and said he didn't know. He begged me to tell him everything that happened last night. Then he saw the ropes that I had pushed off in the floor and was again taken aback. If he was looking for sympathy, he wasn't getting it here.

Evan sobbed so hard I thought he was going to have a heart attack. He went to the kitchen and brought some water and tried to clean me up. The blood was dried, and he scrubbed way too hard. I just lay there. I didn't care if I got clean or not, I just wanted my baby. Evan lifted me off the bed and sat me in a chair while he stripped the bed and put new bed clothes on it. He gently lifted me back to the bed and went and got me some food. I had not had a bite to eat or drink since yesterday. He gave me a drink and fed me a few bites.

I refused to talk to him. I didn't want to hear any apologies. My heart had died about the same time my baby did. I was so empty. Dear God, I have never felt so defeated. I lay there for several hours. I didn't care if I ever got up again. Evan left and was gone for a long time. When he came back, he had some chicken and dumplings for me to eat. I knew he had been to his mother's. I wondered if he had told her anything. In my heart I knew he hadn't. He fed me some and nursed me like he cared. I slept.

Another day Ms. Diary.

December, 1944

*D*ear Ms. Diary,

It's December, and I'm still here trying to get my ducks in a row. I haven't seen Fred. How I would like to be held if only for a few minutes. My soul feels raped of any emotion. I bought a truck, and Evan drives it to work unless I want to use it. One day I may use it to disappear. I've got some money saved, and it's where Evan can't find it. I thank you, Ms. Diary, for taking care of it for me.

Evan has not had anything to drink since that horrible night. He tries so hard to make it up to me, but it's all in vain. I've been stripped of my humanity towards him. I know he has nightmares about the war, and I'm pretty sure he has nightmares about our baby, at least I hope he does. I never mention it, and neither does he. Sometimes he tries to hold me and I cringe. I know he can feel it.

We told Cleve and Doris that the baby was stillborn, and that it was a boy. Evan told me he doesn't remember anything about that night. It's not Evan who I care about; it's his mom and dad. Evan went up on the hill to Nora's grave and came back in such a state I actually felt sorry for him.

It seems my circle of family and friends is much

smaller, and I realize I'm cutting myself off from people. I don't think that's a good thing.

I'm making plans. I will let Cleve know but no one else. I will write to Loretta and the rest of my family after I've relocated. I've sold the farm. Mr. Sias over at Kelsey bought it, but I haven't told Evan yet. I will take the deed and collect the money for it on my way out of town. I've asked Mr. Sias to not say anything to anyone until I'm gone. He agreed.

We'll talk later, Ms. Diary

The Breaking Storm

1945

January 6, 1945

*D*ear Ms. Diary,

I've written Evan a letter to explain what I was doing and told him he would have to pack up and go home to Mommy. I told him he'd blown any chance we had of a life together. It's hard to believe that only three years ago this month I was wide eyed and innocent of the ways of the world, but no longer.

Mr. Sias wants to be in here and ready to plant come spring. I will make that happen. I will leave the letter for Evan because I know he will try and stop me from leaving, and I can't let that happen. Things are almost in place for me to vacate this farm. I'm taking very little with me. I know I can find a furnished room and go from there. Wish I could see Fred and ask him to come with me, but this is not his problem.

I will have a talk with Doris and Cleve, but I'll talk with Cleve first. I plan on being gone by the first of February. I'm going home to see Papa, Grandpa and the boys next weekend. I will be saying goodbye, but they won't know it until much later. I have already stopped by the general store and picked up my dresses and designs. I will start all over on my sewing. Ms. Diary, my head is swimming. There are so many things going round and round in it.

Til tomorrow

February 21, 1945

*D*ear Ms. Diary,
I know we haven't been able to talk lately, but life got in the way. Cleve asked me not to say anything to Doris. He said she would go running to Evan before I'm ready. I suspect he is right.

I did not tell Cleve about Evan and what he had done

about the baby. I did not want him to have that image in his head about his son.

Cleve knows Mr. Sias and will be glad to have him as his neighbor. Cleve understands why I had to sell the property instead of giving it to him. He knows I don't want Evan to get it eventually, and that if he wants something he must work for it like I did.

I will be leaving Thursday morning after I take Evan to work. I'm going over to the feed store today and buy grain as if everything is normal. He doesn't have a clue, or if he does, he hasn't said anything.

I don't know yet where I'm going. I'm going to write a letter to Mr. Dawson for Fred once I get settled. If he wants to come to me, okay, and if not, that's okay, too. I thought I would start driving and see where I end up. When I come to the crossroads in town, maybe I will flip a coin to see if I'm going east or west, north or south. It will be an adventure.

I have all my sewing packed upstairs and my clothes, which are few. There are but few other things I want to take with me.

Ms. Diary, day after tomorrow life will change dramatically for me. I'm almost nineteen and know I should be afraid, but I'm more afraid of staying here. My insides feel like they are dancing to music I've never heard. God, I've neglected you so. I have no right to ask for anything. If you could, give me courage to say goodbye to Cleve, for I know and he knows that it will be the last time we see each other.

Ms. Diary, I may not be able to write to you for a few days, but I will be back.

I have not written Loretta. I will write after I get settled. I'm always afraid she will talk to her husband about the things I tell her now. Maybe I'm selling her short. I don't know. Her husband knows Evan.

I'm so sad to think of leaving my two babies behind and leaving them alone. Ms. Diary, wish me luck and I'll talk to you in a few days.

February, 1945

*D*ear Ms. Diary,

What is wrong with me? I try so hard, and trouble finds me no matter where I hide. I will be nineteen in a few months, and I've already lived a lifetime. How I regret that first letter I wrote to Evan Moore. I was at the feed store today, and Wes Hanson was there. He was a terrible bully when we were in school. He gives me the creeps. He just kept staring at me. I got out of there as fast as I could. I'd only been home for about an hour when I heard a knock on the door; I opened it, and there stood Wes Hanson. He asked if Evan was home, said he would like to talk to him about a job. I explained that Evan was at work in town at the bank. Wes pushed his way into the house. I screamed, and tried to fight but he hit me with his fist. I hit him with a dish that was on the table and cut his eye. He ripped my dress and said he'd always wanted a little piece of squaw. I scratched him in the face and pulled his hair. I spit in his face, and he laughed a sick crazy laugh. After he had his way with me, he laughed and said, "Thank ya, ma'am," tipped his hat and left.

I felt demoralized and dirty. I put water in the wash pan and scrubbed and scrubbed but couldn't get the dirty feeling off. I cried until I had no more tears.

I ran into the bedroom and got the shotgun and fired it after him, even though I knew he was long gone. He won't be for the next shot. He'll be much closer. I sank to the floor, and grief washed over me like a dirty blanket.

Evan came home, and I was still sitting in the floor holding the gun. He asked what happened, and I told him. He was furious. He took the gun from me, and I wrestled him for it. He finally sat, and we talked. I told him we would figure out how to handle it. He held me, and I cried and cried.

I later cleaned up, fixed my hair and told Evan I had an errand to run in town, and I would be taking the truck. He asked why I was taking the shotgun. I explained that you never knew what kind of critter you might run into. He seemed to understand that I needed protection and offered to go with me, I said, "No, I'll take care of it myself."

I stumbled out to the truck as if in a daze. Tomorrow I

am leaving this place. This is not how I planned it. When I made it to the truck, I grabbed the door handle and held on. Nausea overtook me, and my body retched as if trying to vomit out a memory. Oh, God. I had to calm myself and get on with the business of finding Wes Hanson.

When I got to town, I asked if anyone had seen Wes because he had come by looking for work, and we thought we could use him for spring planting. Mr. Dawson said Wes had been in a few minutes ago and looked like he had tangled with a grizzly bear. I asked what happened like I cared. He said Wes had said something about going hunting on Kennard Ridge. I thought that is perfect. He may have a hunting accident. I told Mr. Dawson, "It's not important, I will catch Wes another time," and wished him good day.

I drove up to Kennard Ridge and found his truck. I looked around to try and decide which way he went. I saw some weeds bent over and decided this must be the way. I walked as softly as possible. After a couple of hundred feet, in a big open field next to the edge of the woods I saw his red cap. I found a tree limb to steady my shotgun. I was about to pull the trigger when I heard a shot from right beside me. I saw Wes Hanson fall to the ground. I turned and looked. Evan was standing there beside me. He said he couldn't let me have that on my conscience. I fell into his arms and wept until I couldn't anymore. Ms. Diary, once again life has big changes in store for me. How could I leave Evan now? He's put his life on the line for me.

Evan said he knew in his heart where I was going, and he borrowed his Dad's truck and followed me. He said no one had seen him, and we would go back to the house and decide what to do. I had already decided to be gone by the first of February, and I'm still here. Lordy, Lordy. What now?

When we got back home, we talked for hours and laid all of our cards on the table. He said after that night with the baby, he vowed never to take another drink and he had not. He said he knew I had feelings for Fred and didn't blame me after the way he had treated me. I admitted I did but had never acted on them, and he believed me. I told him about selling the farm and was going to pick the money up on my way out of town Thursday. He looked shocked. Then his face turned red, and then he laughed. He looked at me for several seconds and said, "What am I going to do with you?" He asked if that was still what I wanted to do. It kind of was, but how can you leave a man who has just killed someone for you?

I told him about Mr. Sias, and that I had given my word. He told me maybe if we both went and talked to him he would let me out of my deal. I feel your word is your bond, and you shouldn't take it back. We will talk to Mr. Sias tomorrow.

Ms. Diary, I owe it to my husband to make the best of a bad situation. We'll just have to see where it goes from here. We'll talk tomorrow.

February 25, 1945

*D*ear Ms. Diary,

Evan took off work this morning, this morning when I was supposed to be leaving this place for good. We went and talked to Mr. Sias and told him we'd been through a rough patch and could he possibly release me from our deal. He was very disappointed, but finally agreed. So today Mr. and Mrs. Evan Moore begin life anew. Whatever happens, happens.

Evan said that when it is time for spring plowing he will be the one doing it. He says his leg is fine and aches a little from time to time, but no big deal.

He slept in the same bed as me last night and just held me close. I felt safe. This morning when I fixed his breakfast, I actually wanted to. I have to work around here and sew some today. I must keep my mind and hands busy. I may take all my dresses back to the country store. I made some very good money sewing for the children of the wealthier women. I found I actually liked designing children's clothes. Maybe someday I will have another child. I can't think about that now. Ms. Diary, we will talk tomorrow.

February 27, 1945

*M*s. Diary,

Life is sure getting interesting. Evan came home from work last evening and took care of all the feeding and apologized for not having done that before. Makes me wonder how long that will last. For now, I will just be enjoying it.

Some seed catalogs came in the mail and he sat down and looked through them trying to decide what we will plant in the spring, which is almost here. This morning, when he left for work, he hugged me tightly and kissed me on the cheek and thanked me for being me. He said I was so much better than he deserved and would make it up to me for all the time he was a S.O.B. I told him I didn't think we had that much time. It was a tender moment. I felt a little excitement today for being alive and knowing someone had my back.

I went to the smoke house and got a big beef roast and put it on to cook for the evening meal. I thought we would take some over to his mom and dad later.

Ms. Diary, as long as I can keep my mind busy, I think I can make it.

We'll talk tomorrow.

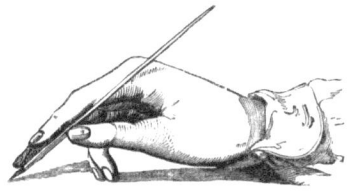

March 14, 1945

Dear Ms. Diary,

I heard at the country store today that Wes Hanson's body had been found. It seems he fell on his gun while out hunting. I gasped when I heard that and tried to keep my composure. It was the last thing I expected. My husband will not be going to jail, and we will never tell another living human being about our secret.

I don't think about Fred very often now, but every once in a while, I remember how it felt to be in his arms and how the cares of the day vanished from my life. So much for young dreams!

When Evan came home, he had already heard at the bank about Wes. I am so sorry that it all happened the way it did. That young man is dead, and I'm responsible. Then I think, no, I'm not! He is! He never should have done what he did, and I never should have done what I did. I'll just have to live with it, and so will Evan. We will have to bury it so deep that it never rises to the surface. Evan and I will never speak of it again.

Ms. Diary, life sure does get complicated, doesn't it?

See you tomorrow

April 11, 1945

*D*ear Ms. Diary,
It's been a while since we've talked. Life is kind of normal here. Evan has been coming in from work at the bank and doing evening chores. He even burned a tobacco bed and a lettuce bed. It's a little late in the year to do that, but better late than never.

Ms. Diary, I've missed my monthly again this month, and I am so scared. I don't think I can survive losing another child. I try to have positive thoughts. Maybe this one will be all right. This baby is due November 29. I want to feel joy, but I'm so scared.

Ms. Diary, do you think other people's lives are this hard? I'm not afraid of hard work, and I don't need much to get along, but how much can the heart take before it just gives out and stops working?

Ms. Diary, we planted potatoes in March along with

some lettuce and green onions. In a few more days we will have wilted lettuce and green onions. I can hardly wait. I decided to take great pleasure in the little things, because the big things seem to elude me.

The war still goes on. How much longer, Lord? How much longer?

Later, Ms. Diary

May 9, 1945

*D*ear Loretta,
It's been a while since I've written. It was good to see you last week and talk for a spell. I trust you to not tell Albert about our conversations.

Loretta, I've been thinking about sitting in your garden. It was almost spiritual. I can still hear the creek whispering on its way to who knows where. I dream of traveling someday, the sweet smell of lilacs, the gentle wind on my face, oh, my! I must come again soon. I was thinking maybe I could make a garden similar to yours. It was uplifting to me. With the war ending last week, it just seems that once again, all's right with the world.

Evan is very different now than he used to be. I just

hope it lasts. If he doesn't drink anymore, it just might. He is a mean drunk. I miss Fred so much, but I am quite content with Evan right now. I guess I should be since I'm going to have another baby.

I know rationing is not over yet and may not be for a few years. I don't understand that, but that's okay. The boys are coming home, and families will be together again. My heart breaks for those who have lost children. I know the pain. Loretta, I am so scared. I can't bear to lose another baby. I keep praying that this time it will be different.

I know when you and Albert have children, it will be a wonderful time in your lives.

I'm still sewing and making wedding dresses. Doris wanted to get out the old layette set we made for Nora and get it ready for this baby since we didn't get to use it for the last one. I haven't been able to do it yet. The baby isn't due until later in the fall. I'm still sewing. It keeps my mind busy. I made seven dresses last week. I'm stashing a portion of the money in case someday I want to run away from home again.

The baby isn't due until November, so I've got plenty of time to get the layette out and work on it. I wish there was a way for me to know if I was going to have a boy or girl. Of course, there isn't, and so it will be a surprise for me just like it is to everyone else.

Evan brought me a beautiful box last Thursday. It looks like carved wood with a fall picture on top under glass and a mirror when you open it up. The picture on top is of a red maple tree losing its leaves, and they are falling in a yard with a little boy and his dog playing in them. I set it on the mantle. Sometimes I look at it, and I know he loves me, and sometimes I look at it, and I don't care if he loves me. I'm such a mess, Loretta. I'll try to be more cheerful in the future.

We are still planting things and preparing to put away berries and things as they come in. I'm looking forward to it. Doris doesn't do a whole lot of canning anymore, so I try to do a little extra for her and Cleve.

Albert has done well by you, and I am so glad.

Loretta, please come by and visit with me sometime. I'm very glad you learned to drive in spite of your mother's protest.

I'm going over to Vonnie's tomorrow for a while and help her with a few things. I love doing that and playing with the children.

I will close for now.

As always, your friend,
Neaaka

September 2, 1945

*D*ear Ms. Diary,

It's been a while since we've talked. Being big with child this summer has taken a lot out of me. We had a huge garden and lots of canning to do. Evan is thinking of quitting the bank and becoming a full-time farmer. He thinks we should apply for a tobacco base, and that would bring in a lot more income. Of course it would also bring a lot of extra work.

Ms. Diary, Evan is doing so good right now. I'm almost afraid to think it might not last. I have to tell you, I still think of Fred and wonder how he's doing.

My baby will be here in two months. I'm excited that I will have time in the winter to enjoy being a mom. Evan will be here for this one, and I hope he loves it as much as I do. I got out Noralyn's layette Saturday and looked at it very carefully. I remember what she looked like in the little smocked dress. I have to muster up some mortar to patch the cracks in my heart as soon as they appear. I miss my precious Nora and my angel baby. God, give me strength. Doris showed me how to do the smocking. I've since done it on some children's dresses. The ladies that I sew for like the smocking very much. I have one wedding dress to finish before October 20, and I'll wait until spring to work on more.

Vonnie came over Sunday with her family, and we cooked dinner together. Our husbands actually seemed to enjoy each other's company. Vonnie, her kids, and I walked up through the woods to the old sulphur spring. Vonnie tripped on a root and rolled over the hill. The children were screaming, and I was trying to see if she was all right. When I found out that nothing was hurt but her pride, I started laughing and could not stop. She looked at me like I was a stranger dropped from the sky. She kept sticking up her hand so I could help her up, and I kept laughing. She had rolled down through a briar patch and was lying under a tree that had fallen a long time ago. I did that same thing many years ago. I guess that's why I thought it was so funny. I laughed so hard I started crying and scared the children. I sat down on the ground and continued to cry. Vonnie got herself up and came to see about me. I had no explanation as to my reaction of her falling. I finally told her it had nothing to do with her falling, that I had been under a lot of pressure this summer and just needed some release. I felt like such an idiot. It's a good thing I have an understanding sister.

Cleve has been real sick. I want so much for him to be here when his grandchild is born.

My papa and grandpa came over last weekend and brought the boys. They are growing up so fast. They are eight and nine now. I guess Papa marrying that old Ellie Parsons was a good thing after all. The boys seem to like her a lot.

I've only been gone from home for almost four years, and it seems like another lifetime ago. It's true once you leave home you can never go back and have things be the same. Ms. Diary, I will say goodnight and we'll talk later.

December, 1945

*D*ear Kalinda,

It's been a long time since I've heard from you; I just wanted to catch you up on what's going on here.

On November 20, Evan and I had a beautiful baby girl. She is very tiny. Mr. Dawson over at the feed store weighed her, and she weighed almost six pounds. I've been carrying her on a pillow.

Evan is scared to death of her. I tried to tell him she wouldn't break. He's only held her once, but I think when she gets a little bigger he will be fine. Her name is Arletta LeeAnn. I've already found myself calling her Letty. Ella Pinson let me borrow her bassinet again. I'm so afraid, Kalinda.

This is my third child. Having lost two already, I can't bear the thought of losing another one. I don't mean to borrow trouble, but my luck seems to run bad.

Evan went out to the barn and brought in the bed that

Cleve had made for Noralyn. It hurt so much to see it and remember her sweet smile. She would be three years old now. When I think of her, it's like a vine wraps around my heart and squeezes until I can hardly breathe.

Vonnie told me you have a boyfriend now. Sure would like to know more about him. Is this someone who just came home from the war?

Kalinda, you're almost twenty-two years old now. I thought you were going to be an old maid. Vonnie tells me you like working for that department store. I've never been in a big store like that. Maybe when Letty is a little older, we will come for a visit.

Letty is almost a month old now. She smiles and looks around; she probably wonders what she has gotten into. She has black hair and big brown eyes. It looks like her hair is going to be curly like mine.

Cleve is doing some better. He comes over every day or two to see the baby. He holds her and sings to her and tells her stories. I wish she could remember them. I will try and remember them so I can tell her again when she is older.

It will be Christmas in a few days. We aren't doing much of anything about it except going to church and praying. I've been able to do that again lately. For some time, it was very foreign. Sometimes our sins, well my sins, just overwhelmed me. Don't ask me what they are because I won't tell you.

Evan goes to church with me, and I like that very much.

Kalinda, do you ever wish we were kids again, and Momma was here, and life was simple? I feel so old sometimes. I think you were wise not to marry young, but I was in such a hurry, and I don't know for what.

I would love for you and your beau to come visit. I get so lonely here. There's always plenty of work to do, and I do it, but I would like to do something else for a change. I feel restlessness in my soul and it scares me.

Well, I've been rambling for a while, so I will close and say goodbye until another day.

> Love to my sister,
> Neaaka

Finding New Wings

1946

January, 1946

$\mathcal{D}$ear Ms. Diary,

It's been a while since we've talked. I have a lot of stuff to tell you. My heart should be so happy. I've got a beautiful baby girl, Evan is being a good husband, he loves me, and most of the time, I'm pretty sure I love him. But I still remember how it felt when Fred put his arms around me. I wonder what he is doing, but I'm afraid to find out. What if he married someone else? Of course if he's happy, I should be glad. I guess I'm just selfish.

Ms. Diary, I feel so sad in my heart. I was in town during Christmas and ran into Mrs. Hanson. Her face told me she loved and missed her son so much. She looked much older than I remembered. She's a mother just like me; she lost her child. The only difference is I took her child in a fit of anger. As I watched her, I realized it didn't matter that he was a rapist and a bully, he was her son, and she loved him. She looked so sad. I wanted to run up to her and tell her how sorry I was about her son, but I couldn't move. I stood there like a cold unmoving stone. A lady at the store asked if she could help me, and it kind of brought me out of my stupor.

Ms. Diary, life should be simple. So why isn't it? I should be sewing every day and playing with Letty and cooking meals for my husband and be happy with that. There is an emptiness inside me that can't be filled. I don't even know what I want to fill it with.

I've read all the books Doris has. I've borrowed books from people, and I've read magazines. I think there's a whole world out there ,and I want to be a part of it. I've heard that some people now have something called telephones in their homes, and they call and talk to their neighbors without having to run over to their house. I feel like the world is starting to change so fast.

I found a fashion magazine at the general store and bought it. I have started making some of the designs and creating some of my own. I noticed when I was doing that, I felt so alive. I put two of the dresses in the general store, and they sold the first day. I got orders for four more. It looks like this may be a busy winter after all. I got a new

National Bella Hess catalog in the mail, and I have made Letty some new clothes. Doris thinks I'm spoiling her, and that's okay with me. Still, when evening comes, I sometimes feel so sad. What do you think is going on, Ms. Diary? Guess I won't wait on the answer.

Until next time

January, 1946

*D*ear Ms. Diary,

So many feelings are going around in my head, or my heart, wherever it is that feelings go. I don't know. I woke up this morning angry. I couldn't figure out why. I was nursing Letty and thinking that my momma probably held me like this and loved me. She must have touched my face and looked into my eyes. She probably ran her fingers over my head and told me how pretty I was. I want her to still do that. The anger was overwhelming. It dawned on me then, I was so, so mad at my momma for dying when I needed her so much. I need her to tell me everything is going to be all right.

Ms. Diary, do you think our lives are all planned before we are born and we have no choice in how it all ends?

Well, I don't. I trust that God will let us make our own decisions and will be there to pick up the pieces when we fail. Apparently, I'm getting pretty good at failing.

I would like to just once sit in the driver's seat of my own life, instead of being someone's daughter, someone's wife, someone's mother, someone's dishwasher, and someone's everything else. Just let me sit in the driver's seat of my own life for a little while. I'm so tired. I've got to snap out of this funk I'm in. Evan tries so hard to cheer me up, but it just irritates me. I still want to just pick up and go but where and why? What would I be running away from, and what would I be running to? Nothing. That's what, on both counts. Maybe a good night's sleep will help. Yeah, that's going to happen with a two-month-old to take care of. Evan would never even think of getting up with the baby, after all that is woman's work. Bullshit.

I thought after the war was over all would be right with the world, but nothing has changed except there are more men around.

Evan says he is definitely quitting the bank in the spring when it's planting time and is going to be a farmer. His dad is very happy, and his mother is throwing a fit. She's proud that her son is a *banker* to hear her tell it. Never mind he's just a teller and does what he's told, or that he hates it.

Tomorrow, when I get up, it's going to be a brand-new day, and I'm going to decide to be happy and make life worthwhile. I will love my baby and try real hard to love

Evan. I will sew and make some money. It will be wonderful.

Yeah, who am I kidding? Life goes on.

Later, Ms. Diary

April 3, 1946

*D*ear Loretta,

It's been some time since I've written. Seems like nothing ever changes here, but yet change is constant. Evan quit the bank and is going to farm this summer. Heaven, help us. I don't think he knows which end of the plow to blow on.

If I didn't have Letty, I would go find a job and get away from home. I feel so discontented, and I really don't know why. Most all the women I know seem content to stay home and be a wife and mother. I have an itch in my soul that makes me want to go places and do things other than work here at home. Do you think that makes me a bad person?

I am so honored that you named your little girl after me. Laura Mae has a nice ring to it. My mother's name was Nyoka Mae, and mine is Neaaka Mae, so Mae goes on. She is so pretty.

Vonnie has two children now. She and Jim seem very happy, but she's never had this wanderlust that I feel.

I'm working on some new designs for dresses and I saw in a magazine where they are having some kind of show in Memphis for new designers. I thought I might make a wedding gown, and some house dresses, and maybe a bathing suit and go down to Memphis. Doris thinks my designs are scandalous. I think she's too old-fashioned.

I thought I would ask Evan what he thinks about it, but then I thought he would say I had no business going anywhere. I decided to tell him that I was going, and that turned out to be the best. He still argued but soon saw that my mind was made up. I don't seem to be like other people, and I can't decide if that is a good or a bad thing. What do you think, Loretta?

I still think about Fred and wonder what life would have been like if I had left on the day my world stood still. I know you don't know what I'm talking about, and I am being overly dramatic.

I discovered a little place down by the creek last summer where I could go and commune with God. I think He's not happy with me most of the time. I am a blatant sinner who always seems to need redeeming. I don't mean to be. I try to do what's right, and I'm just not very good at it. I have a bitter feeling for Doris sometimes, and I know that's not right, but that woman irks my soul. You know how she treated me when Evan left for the army. I'm trying to get past it.

I cooked some leather britches yesterday and took some over to them. Cleve, of course, told me how good they were, and enjoyed them immensely. Doris, on the other hand, had to find something wrong with them. This time they needed a little more salt. She certainly doesn't need any more salt, she's sour enough!

I asked her if she would watch Letty while I went to Memphis in June. She started coming up with all the reasons why she couldn't. Cleve said, yes, they would be glad to take her for a couple of days.

When I get my designs done I may bring them over for you to see. You have a good eye and are not an old fogey.

Will go for now. Hope to see you soon.

Yours Truly,
Neaaka

June 21, 1946

*D*ear Ms. Diary,
I'm so excited I can hardly contain myself. I took my designs and the finished products to the show in Memphis, The judges liked them! They actually liked them! They wanted to talk to me about doing more designs and selling them to a company, and they would make the product and market it and pay me a royalty— whatever that is.

They gave me a lot of paperwork to read. I read it very carefully, although I'm betting they thought I wouldn't. One of the judges thought my wedding gown was beautiful but a little too risqué. She reminded me of Doris. Here I go sinning again.

Evan didn't seem at all excited about my new adventure. That's okay. I'm excited enough for both of us. My wedding dress was a just-below-the-knee design, and they want me to do a full-length with a train. I've been working on the design, and it is gorgeous.

When I was at the show and saw all the beautiful work, I was starstruck. I didn't feel like a country bumpkin anymore.

They said my house dresses were very pretty and practical, and that women would love them. I even made a couple of aprons to match. I don't know what kind of money I will make, and I almost don't care. Well, I care a little bit. I'm sure it will help supplement the farm. Glad I could share some good news with you.

Until next time, Ms. Diary.

August 2, 1946

*D*ear Vonnie,

I am so excited to tell you my designs for my dresses have been picked up by Haven and Sons Co. When I took the wedding dress in with the train, they offered me one hundred dollars cash for it. I've never made money like that. They will buy my designs and make the dresses. I will still design and sew for people around here.

They are going to photograph the wedding dress for some kind of magazine. They think they will get a lot of orders from it.

Vonnie, I must come over soon and see you and the kids. I'm sure they are growing like weeds. Speaking of weeds, Evan is trying to get the crops in and I'm canning something every day. Our cellar is getting full.

Do you think there will ever come a time when women

will wear pants a lot? I know some of the hoity toity women do, I've seen them in magazines.

I'm a very busy woman right now, with a baby, drawing, canning, cooking, laundry, and such.

I wish I could say I was happy and content, but there is a nagging feeling I'm supposed to be doing more or something different. I don't know what this restlessness I feel is, but I wish it would go away.

I'm going back to Memphis in November for another show. I've been thinking about something. I would like to design pants for women. I could make them out of gabardine, and they would look very nice. Well, it's just an idea.

Must run for now. Will come over or write soon.

Neaaka

November 19, 1946

*D*ear Ms. Diary,

The most dreadful thing has happened. I went to Memphis for a designer's show. I've been so excited about my work as a designer. I walked into a five-and-dime store and saw Fred standing at a counter. He didn't see me at first, but all my old feelings came rushing back like a raging sea. I wanted to run, but my feet seemed glued to the floor. I prayed he wouldn't turn around and see me.

It felt like there was a movie playing in my head. I remembered the first time I saw him and the first time he held me. I wanted it all again. I knew I couldn't walk through a door that I had nailed shut, so I turned and ran. I saw him turn just as I did, and I don't know if he recognized me and followed me or not. At first, I hoped he did, and then I hoped he didn't. Once your heart has been broken, does it grow back bigger or does the crack get wider? For a while I couldn't think. It felt like ocean waves crashing against my brain. I stumbled into the store next door and went into their restroom. I knew he wouldn't find me there. I waited for more than thirty minutes and then cautiously walked out. I didn't see him anywhere, so I went back to the show, but couldn't keep my mind on anything.

I read all the papers Mr. Haven gave me, and it sounded like I was not getting a very good deal, so I didn't sign them. I wondered if I was shooting myself in the foot, but I was so rattled from seeing Fred I didn't care. They were buying my designs, which was good, but they were making all the money from them. It didn't seem right to me, and of course, I told them so. They were taken aback that I had the nerve to question men and their decisions. I felt like I should get a percentage of every dress they made and sold using my designs. I asked a lot of questions, and when they answered, I ripped their answers to shreds. Soon though, they digested them and thought maybe they could give me a small percentage. I insisted on the option to up my percentage if sales increased dramatically. I told a little white lie, and said I had a lawyer look the contract over. The truth is I sank my talons into those pages, and what I didn't understand I looked up at the library. Here I go sinning again.

Fred is still casting shadows on my mind, and I need the sun desperately to make them go away. I drove back to Mason in a daze. It's a wonder I found my way home. I felt changed somehow, but I couldn't put my finger on it. I'm just a confused mess. It's probably all this sinning and lying I've been doing.

Ms. Diary, when I got up this morning, I looked around here. I saw a farm, a good farm, with everything we need to work it. Evan is working so hard, and he's being a good husband, much better than I deserve. I have a beautiful baby girl. I should be so happy. What's wrong with me? I would settle for a little contentment.

I have so many ideas on so many things. Maybe I should write them down. Ideas are like wings, don't you think? Sometimes they just take off and fly on their own. Sometimes they are but a fleeting shadow on a cloudy day. Oh well, Ms. Diary, tomorrow is another day.

Neaaka

Shadows on the Horizon

1947

January 17, 1947

*D*ear Ms. Diary,

      I expect you are sick of hearing me whine. I know I am. Evan and I took Letty to church this morning. The preacher preached straight at me. It was like he saved up everything I ever thought and threw it out at me today. He talked about the tongue being a two-edged sword and how it could hurt people. I know that. I've been cut a few times with that sword. He said it doesn't matter what we put into our mouth, it's what comes out that counts. He reminded me that the tongue is but a bucket, and the heart is the well. Whatever spews out of that bucket or *tongue* is what is stored up in the heart. It made sense and made my heart feel dirty. I'll think twice about going back next Sunday. Who knows, maybe that's what I need. I don't see much point in doing anything anymore. Vonnie told me I have a bad case of *can't help its*. I asked what that was and she said sometimes when a woman has a baby, they go through a bad time for a few months, and they can't help it.

Ms. Diary, did you ever hear of such a thing? I don't want to talk anymore. Thanks for listening.

June 17, 1947

D ear Ms. Diary,

It's June and most things are planted, Evan works very hard. I am so proud of him, and I try to be a good wife. I really do. I know I don't deserve everything I have, especially after today.

I was sewing on a dress, and someone knocked on the door. Evan was out in the fields. At first I was startled, because nobody ever knocks. They just walk in and holler. I went to open the door, and there stood Fred. I had not seen nor heard from him since I saw him in Memphis last year. I stared at him, and my heart almost beat out of my chest. He saw me as no other eyes have ever seen me. He looked into my soul. Neither of us spoke. Then he looked past me and saw Letty playing on the floor, and his eyes drifted down to my six-month belly. He backed up slowly on the porch and grabbed onto the post. He slowly and softly said, "I love you, Neaaka," and I knew it was goodbye and I would never see him again. I bowed my head to hide my tears. When I looked up again, he was gone. I stood there and tried to stifle the scream that wanted to be released. I could not. I didn't want to scare Letty, so I stepped out onto the porch for a minute. I screamed like a panther, and then sobbed quietly.

I looked at Letty and smiled even though my heart was breaking. I picked her up and held her close. I dwelt on my memories for a long time. I walked out to the barn and stood in the spot where he first held me when I was so scared. I remembered our one and only kiss. I remembered how we could talk, and talk, and talk. I remembered the butterflies that flew around in my tummy when he was near. I kept fanning the embers to keep them alive; I couldn't bear their death, not yet.

I keep telling myself I have not been unfaithful to Evan, but in my heart I knew I had. I never will again. I opened the door and stepped back into my life. I will always stay on this side of goodbye.

The only thing I can do now is put Fred in the past and keep him there. When I think of him, I will stop and think of something else. I will raise my children and love my husband. I will, I will. I must. Tomorrows another day, Ms. Diary.

June 24, 1947

*D*ear Ms. Diary,

You would think not much can happen in a day, but it can. I'm not the same person today that I was yesterday.

I lay there last night courting sleep that would not come. I had some time to do some powerful thinking. Evan lay beside me so tired from his day's work. He had his back to me and seemed to be sleeping peacefully. I placed my hand on his shoulder and listened to him breathe. I wonder if it is possible to love two men at the same time. I remembered what now seems like a lifetime ago, how he was all that I wanted. I have him now, he's a good man, and works so hard for us. He reminds me sometimes that I bought this farm. I guess it still bothers him, but it shouldn't. It's our home and always will be. I have set my mind to it, and nothing will change it. Do you hear me? Nothing. It's too bad life doesn't come with an eraser so we could be mistake free, but I guess that's what makes us who we are.

Our new baby is due in September. I hope it's a little boy, but it doesn't matter really as long as it's healthy. This will be my fourth child. I have to stop thinking about my lost children. The sadness is unbearable.

Papa, Ellie, Grandpa and the boys are coming over for Sunday dinner after church. I guess I deserve to go back and let the preacher preach at me. Luke and Levi are young men now. Well, not really, but they sure have grown a lot. It will be fun to spend some time with them.

I feel like I should apologize to Ellie, but, since she didn't know how I felt, she wouldn't know what I was talking about. I guess I will let it go. She did turn out to be very nice, and she makes Papa happy. Even Grandpa likes her.

I got a check in the mail today for seventy-two dollars. It was a royalty check for the dresses Haven sold. The letter said there would be another check next week. A good wife would tell her husband there was extra money, and he would come up with something to spend it on. Well, I guess I'm not that good of a wife yet. I will save it for hard times.

It looks like there is some kind of blight on the tomatoes. I'm not sure if there's anything that can be done or not, neither is Evan. We were planning on canning at least a hundred quarts.

Ms. Diary, Evan still asks about you once in a while. Last time I answered his question with a question. He said, "Are you still writing your thoughts down in that diary?"

I said, "Does it look like I have time to have thoughts, let alone write them down?"

He laughed and said, "Yeah, I guess you're right."

He wanted to know where the old one was that I wrote in when he was gone to war. I said it's around here some-place. I'm sure we'll come across it someday. He seemed satisfied with that. Is skirting around the truth the same as lying? Okay, I know it is. See you soon, Ms. Diary.

October 22, 1947

*D*ear Ms. Diary,

Evan and I are the parents of a precious little boy. He is one month old today. His name is Silas Samuel Moore. We are very proud of him. He has dark skin and black hair like me but blue eyes like Evan.

As much joy as I feel in my heart today, I have enough sadness to match. You see, my confidant, my buddy, the one who always believed in me, passed away two weeks ago. The world is a much sadder place without Grover Cleveland Moore. The wound that is left feels like it will never heal. I had Doris watch the children for a little while yesterday. I just wanted to walk up the creek on the farm and remember Cleve. He never made me feel like an idiot little hill girl. I remembered when he dressed Doris down for hiding Evan's letters from me and the time he helped me drag Evan out to the back porch knowing he wouldn't remember how he got there. He was always fair-spoken and never pretentious.

I hope Silas grows up exactly like him. I remembered him coming to the barn the week after Evan and I were married. I was sitting on an upside down bucket milking the cow. About the time he walked in, the cow flipped her tail and knocked me off the bucket into a cow pile. He tried so hard not to laugh, and I was so embarrassed. I started to laugh, and he couldn't hold it any longer. I have so many great memories of him.

I sure wish I could say the same of Doris. I had to lie down for a little while before I could take the kids home. Doris seemed a little concerned about me, but I doubt she is. Lord, I'm feeling the meanness creeping in, please forgive me.

Doris acts like she's totally helpless and depends on Evan for everything. I understand that, I really do, but it's so hard for him.

When I feel better, I will help her and take some of the load off him. I've been coughing a lot lately and not feeling well. I walked out to the barn one day last week and was so tired I could hardly make it back. Evan wants me to see Dr. Green, and I will soon.

Letty thinks Silas is a doll and wants to play with him.

I caught her trying to feed him a dill pickle. He was not impressed.

Luke and Levi are coming over this weekend to help Evan with some of the farm work. Even though it's winter, there are still things to be done—mostly repairs on farm equipment so it will be ready in the spring. It will be so good to see my baby brothers. Ms. Diary, I will talk to you again soon.

December 9, 1947

*D*ear Loretta,

So good to see you at Cleve's wake, and thank you for the chicken and dumplings. They were very good. I was surprised that you had learned to cook.

We buried Cleve next to Noralyn Mae. There was a chill in the air that I can't explain. It hurt my bones, or maybe it hurt my heart, and I only thought it was my bones. The sky was overcast like a darkness that was creeping into my soul. I can't believe Cleve is gone. The Bible says, "To be absent from the body is to be present with the Lord." If that's the case, I know he will take care of my heavenly babies. Maybe it's the sadness that's sapping the strength from my body, but I can't see how that would make me cough like I do. I think I just have a cold.

Old Mr. Dunbar down at the bank said I sounded like I had consumption. It startled me, but I tried not to think any more about it, but every now and then the thoughts creep in, and it scares me. I have two babies. If I have consumption, who would take care of them? I'm trying to think positive. Right now I'm just positive that I'm sick and have no time to lie down.

Evan came in from town today and said he was thinking about getting Hettie Gamble's daughter Sarah to come and help me out until I started feeling better. My first thought was I could lie down. How bad is that? I should be saying I will care for my own children, and my own husband, and my own home, but I couldn't. I'm too sick.

Feeling bad,
Neaaka

The Afterglow

1948

January 17, 1948

*D*ear Ms. Diary,

This is not how I planned for my life to go. Doris has had my babies now for two weeks, and I haven't been able to see them. I went to see Dr. Green last month, and he is supposedly watching me. He said I may have consumption, but he's not sure. He wanted me to go to a sanitarium. I refused because if he is not sure, and if I went, I would be exposed to something I may not have. Doctors can be so ignorant sometimes. He was not impressed when I told him that, but he'll get over it.

Sarah has been here for over a week now. She's only

seventeen and works very hard. She's so pretty it takes my breath away. I wonder what it does to Evan.

Ms. Diary, I feel so alone. I know God is with me. In my heart, I know this. It does not feel tangible right now. Evan is afraid of me. I really do understand this, but it is so lonely. Both he and Sarah wear a handkerchief over their face when they come into my room. I feel like I have leprosy.

I can see the front room from my bedroom. I can see Sarah and Evan laughing and talking. I can't always hear what they say. I know they are enjoying each other's company. It disturbs me quite a bit. I'm not sure I have the right to be disturbed considering what all I'm putting him and Doris through. There was a time when I wouldn't have cared if I had that right or not, maybe one day that girl will come back, maybe she won't, I don't know. Don't feel like writing any more. Dr. Green has been giving me some medicine and some days I feel better. He's made some kind of test to see if I really have consumption. It may be another month or so before I know.

My babies are so little they may not know me when I get to see them again.

Ms. Diary, I have to apologize for the places I have to hide you now. When I'm better I will give you a good bath.

March 22, 1948

*D*ear Ms. Diary,

It's been four nightmarish months since I've seen my babies. There's a nightmare going on in my own home, also. I'm now determined to get better. Dr. Green still has not given me any results of my test, and it's been months.

Well Ms. Diary, let me tell you what's been going on. Sarah has been going over to Doris's sometimes to help with the children. My children!

I was watching Sarah and Evan sitting in the living room one evening talking. They kept looking back toward the bedroom. They knew I could see them, then one at a time they got up and went toward the kitchen out of sight.

The feeling I had made me want to throw up. I wasn't born yesterday. The following week they decided it would be a good idea to change the furniture around in my room. I said no, but they did it anyway. They better hope I don't get well. However, they were too stupid to realize they set the dresser where the bed used to be, which gave me a terrific view. I finally realized if I was going to get better, I would have to do it on my own. If they have kept me away from my babies, and I don't have anything contagious, they can consider themselves and Dr. Green dead meat!

I have started to sit up on my bed and let my feet hang

over. I wiggle my feet and toes, and shake my legs, and stretch my arms. Every time one of them catches me, they make me lie back down. My cough is almost gone, and I feel okay, just weak. I'm weak from lying here so much. I will gain my strength back even if I have to exercise during the night. I really don't need much care now, so why is Sarah still here? I can get up and use the chamber pot. She was very surprised by that. She acted like she was tickled to death that I was getting better, but there was an undercurrent that I noticed. I don't trust her or Evan.

Two days ago, I was lying in my bed with my eyes closed. When I opened them I could see Sarah and Evan kissing in the front room through the mirror that they so graciously placed there for me. I started the dry heaves, but I had nothing to throw up.

They both came running as if they were innocent and caring. I stood up and really surprised them, and told Sarah to get out, and told Evan he may not live to see the morning. They were convinced I was losing my mind, and I knew I had found it. My head hurt. I couldn't think.

Soon as Sarah left, I made Evan leave also for a while. I told him to go check on the children, then if he had enough nerve he could come back and stay till morning. I had no intentions of sleeping. I slowly felt my old self coming back. I wonder how she got away from me like this.

All night long I tried to formulate a plan; of what, I don't know. I have to see Fred—I have to see Fred. I have no idea where he is or how I would get in touch with him. I need to see him badly.

It's March already and getting time to burn tobacco beds and start turning the winter crops under. I feel desperate for some reason. They still won't let me see my children, and I'm not strong enough to walk over there or drive at this point.

I just found out that Sarah is staying at Doris's and helping take care of my babies. I'm gonna have to kill somebody, I do believe.

I spend the days walking through the house and trying to get my strength built up. Today I'm going to attempt the stairs. I will walk up them and sit and scoot down them. I don't want to take a chance of falling. Evan has to help his mom so much more now that Sarah is there. Shit!

Talk to you later, Ms. Diary

April 16, 1948

*D*ear Ms. Diary,

Today is a new day. I'm feeling so much better. The doctor stopped by to see me. I said, "I'll bet you're surprised to see me up and about aren't you?"

He looked at me and said, "Why no, I expected you to be up. I told Evan you did not have consumption, that it was a lung infection, and that last medicine should have made a big difference. I just stopped by to make sure." He said I had never been a danger to my children. My knees buckled, and I fell and caught myself on the table. The doctor came to steady me and help me to sit down. My mind was muddy, I couldn't think. What was going on? I need some time to think.

I guess I can't just kill Evan, can I? But I can give him some sacred bark. Yes, I can! I'll make him a nice cup of tea. It will give him a case of the trots he won't soon forget. I think it couldn't happen to a nicer guy.

After the doctor left, I decided not to tell Evan that he stopped by. Evan was plowing out on knob hill. My head was throbbing with my new information. I have to do something, but what? I need to think, but I'm too angry. I got the keys to the truck and drove over to Doris's. I'm glad it wasn't very far. I got angrier as I drove. I'm not sure what their plan is, but they have messed with the wrong woman.

I walked up to the door, opened it and walked in. Sarah was sitting in the floor playing with my kids. She and Doris looked at me like they were horrified. I told Sarah to get her things and get out. She was no longer needed. Doris said, "You can't come into my house and tell someone to leave." I looked at her with a determination that I'm sure she'd never seen before. I said, "Get away from my children." The children started crying, I knew I was scaring them, but I couldn't help it. I picked Silas up and got Letty by the hand. They were both screaming. I felt so bad. I had to get them out of there. I would get their clothes later. As I walked out the door, I told Doris to get their things packed, and I would pick them up tomorrow. Doris was yelling at me the whole time. I asked the Lord to keep his hand over my mouth until I got out of there.

I put the babies in the truck. Silas is old enough now to sit up, however, he didn't know anything about holding on. I laid him in the truck seat and sat Letty in front of him and told her to hold on.

Instead of going home I went to the feed store to see Mr. Dawson. I asked about Fred. I had no shame. He said he was still working in Memphis. I blatantly asked for his address. I then went to the general store to get some sacred bark. We'll see how Evan likes to sit on the throne. It's almost spring, and I'm sure he could use a good physic, and it tastes better than castor oil.

The one thing I'm not feeling today is sacred. I need to take a deep breath and hug my babies. They don't even know me. I'm pretty sure I hate Evan. Okay, Okay, calm down.

Ms. Diary, I'm afraid of myself right now. I have to think. I must think.

March 24, 1948

*D*ear Ms. Diary,

It's been four days now since I took my kids back. I guess I've calmed down a little, but I'm still so angry. Evan came over two nights ago, knocked on the door and asked if he could come in. I told him he didn't live here anymore. He said he figured that. He just wanted to talk, but I had no desire to hear anything he had to say. I couldn't imagine what he was thinking. Does he not know me? He's lucky he's still in an upright position. He tried explaining how and why he was so taken with Sarah. He said she was so young, beautiful, and kind—and so good with the kids. I guess I am getting old, I'm twenty-one now. I feel so much older. I know life is hard, but this hard. Really?

I let him talk and never said a word. He didn't quite know how to handle that. He expected me to argue, but I had other plans. I had already gone to see Mr. Sias to see if he still wanted to buy the farm, and he did. I had already started packing things up and getting ready to move. I had received three more checks from Haven; they are still selling my designs and wanting more. I can do that anywhere. I have no idea where I'm going, but I'm going. I thought once, and only once, that I wasn't being fair, taking the kids and leaving, but he had no problem taking them from me and lying to me about it.

When he came over he did not ask to see Silas and

ignored Letty when she hugged his leg. I will not be telling him I'm leaving and asked Mr. Sias not to say anything about buying the farm until I told him to. When I didn't say anything, he was looking frightened and kept watching me and didn't sit down. I watched him and never said a word. I knew I was making him very nervous, and that was my intention. He said, "Well, I reckon I'd better go." I nodded my head and agreed with him. He left a very puzzled man. I put Letty to bed and tried to make some sense out of this mess and tried to decide the rest of my life.

My brain felt like a spinning top and I had to lie down. I guess I must have dozed off. Someone knocked on the door, and I got up to answer it thinking Evan had come back. He hadn't. Lo and behold, there stood Fred, straight and tall like a punctuation mark. My life finally made sense even though we hadn't seen each other or talked for a long time. I walked straight into his arms, and I never wanted to be anywhere else.

We talked well into the night. I couldn't help but wonder why he showed up right at that moment. He said he hadn't been able to get me off his mind for a few weeks and when he saw his uncle, Joe Dawson, and found out that I had asked about him, he had to see me. He didn't know whether or not Evan would be there, but assumed he would and was quite relieved when he wasn't.

He told me he was working for a factory in Memphis and was making decent money and had been able to save some. He had rented a nice little house that could use a woman's touch. I asked if he remembered I had two children. He said they were a part of me, and we would all be fine. He gave me his address and directions to his place. I said I needed a couple of weeks to get things done here. So now, I have to add a divorce to my resume. I will see a lawyer tomorrow.

Well, it's off to bed, but no sleep for me.

Later, Ms. Diary

April 24, 1948

*D*ear Ms. Diary,

You are my one true friend. I've told you things I wouldn't dream of telling anyone else. You've always kept my confidences and never let me down. I know Evan still wonders about you, but so far, we've been able to keep you safe, or should I say keep me safe.

I took the children over to Vonnie's today and left them with her while I went over to Salem and saw a lawyer. I had to tell Vonnie all that had been going on, and she was shocked but agreed that I should do something.

The lawyer said I didn't have grounds for divorce

unless Evan had committed adultery. I told him about Sarah, and that the Bible said if he had lusted for someone he had committed adultery in his heart already. I truly don't believe they have, but didn't want the lawyer to know that. I told him about all the time they were alone in my house and certainly could have and about my seeing a reflection of them in the mirror and how they moved back out of my sight. He said he would file the paperwork, and it would take about a year. I was outraged! I told him it would take one week, or I would find another lawyer. He tried explaining that these things take time. I was having none of it. I had been saving my money from Haven and had cash.

When he found that out, he was not going to let me go without some resolution. I told him I was moving to Memphis, and I could get a lawyer there. He tried to convince me that I did not want a big-city lawyer. I already knew that. My head and my heart are somehow out of sync. I can't seem to get them working together. I couldn't understand why it was so easy to get married and so hard to get a divorce. I knew I was going to be painted a scarlet woman for leaving my husband. I wondered if I should care, or maybe I'm past that now.

The lawyer took care of the paperwork and said it would be a year before I could marry again. That was okay with me. My reputation was already ruined. I have been taught that when you make your bed, you are the one who has to lie in it. I would only pay him half of what he asked; I told him he could have the rest when I was a free woman. I asked him to wait two weeks to send the papers to Evan. I can get a lot done in two weeks. I would like to see Evan and Doris's face when they get the papers, because I named Sarah as correspondent. Let them put that in their pipe and smoke it! Okay, my brain is in a fog.

My heart doesn't know where the hell it is, and I am so mad at the whole situation and even madder when I realize I still care for Evan. I keep telling myself I will not back down. I will not. Evan is the father of my children. What right do I have to take his children away from him? Isn't that what he was going to do to me?

Ms. Diary, tomorrow is another day and will come with enough trouble of its own. I must say goodnight or some such rot to somebody, so I guess you're it. Good night and see you tomorrow.

April 26, 1948

*D*ear Ms. Diary,

Has it only been eight years since I started writing to Evan? I don't think I will let Letty learn to write. It would have saved me so much heartache and trouble.

234

Evan still has not been over to see the children; he had better get a move on.

Mr. Sias gave me the money for the farm, and I have signed the deed over to him. He has given me the time I need to get things done, but it is spring, and Evan has already done some plowing and Mr. Sias needs to get to work on his planting, so I have to talk with Evan. I wasn't going to tell him anything, just disappear, but I have to do what's right as much as I can. I don't have any idea what to say to him. I know he thinks I'm going to knuckle down and stay right here and work my hiney off, and nothing is going to change. He's wrong, of course. Everything is going to change, and that's on him not me!

I'm not taking a lot with me, just personal things and my sewing equipment. I've made a few things lately for the general store, so I have that money, and I've sold some more designs to Haven. Designing is what I do when I'm frustrated and wanting to do or be someone different.

I know that's wrong, and that I should be happy with the hand I've been dealt. Someday I will, but not today.

Evan came by the house today on his Dad's tractor. I stopped him and said we need to talk. Then I said no, I need to talk, and you need to listen. So he is coming over later this evening after the kids are down for the night. He did not ask if he could come earlier and see them. I can't even begin to guess what he's thinking.

We'll talk later, Ms. Diary

April 30, 1948

*D*ear Ms. Diary,

Well, Evan came over last night. When he came in, he stood at the door. I asked him to sit down. He reluctantly pulled a chair over fairly close the door. I said, "Evan, I have no plans to shoot you. Relax."

"Evan, the only way I know how to do things is to be straight up about it. So here's what going on," I blurted out. Once I got going, I couldn't stop until I was finished. "You have hurt me deeply, and I can never trust you or live with you again." He started to say something. I told him his job was to listen until I was through and then he could talk as long as he wanted.

I said, "When I saved money and bought this farm while you were away at war, I meant it to be our home for as long as we were on this earth. I meant for our children to grow up here, and our grandchildren to run and play, and wade in the creek, and climb the hills. But you took that away because of a pretty face, and you tried to steal my children, children that you have never even been over to see in weeks. What were you thinking? Were you going to kill me and have a nice little life with Sarah and my children? You are at the next farm over. You could be here in ten minutes walking."

He started to say something again and I stopped him. "My turn still. You let me think I was a danger to them knowing that I wasn't. How could you do something like that? It seems that I don't know you at all. I can see you take after your mom and not your dad. That's too bad. So this is what's going to happen."

He looked at me questioning, not knowing what to say, if anything.

"I have sold the farm to Mr. Sias." He gasped, but said nothing. The shocked look on his face was priceless.

"He's already paid me. And I'm using that money to buy another place in Memphis. I've also filed for divorce. It will be final one year from now. Neither of us can remarry until then. I will keep sewing for the general store and designing for Havens. You can see the children on a regular basis if you want to. You won't need to do any more farm work here. Mr. Sias will be here on Tuesday to start his plowing. You can close your mouth now. Your turn."

Tomorrow's another day, Ms. Diary

April 30, 1948

*D*ear Ms. Diary,

Evan had his turn talking last night. His first response was to pick up the chair he was sitting in and crash it against the floor. His face and neck were so red. I think he was trying to scare me, and he did, but I never let on. I wouldn't give him the satisfaction. He asked me who I thought I was. He said other women stay home and take care of their families and wanted to know why I couldn't be like them. He said I thought I was something because I could earn money and not have to depend on him.

I thought, there it is. There's the rub, the source of contention. No man wants a wife who can take care of herself. I promise, Ms. Diary, I never thought of it like that. I wanted it for us, not just me. When I didn't react or speak he finally calmed down. He sat and stared at the floor for a long time and said nothing. Finally, he said, "Neaaka, I don't even know where to begin. I don't know how we got to this point. I thought we were happy. Then you got so sick. I honestly thought you weren't going to make it. I guess I forgot who I was dealing with." He looked up at me and grinned that crooked little grin that I love. He was still furious I could tell. I knew then he was putting on an act, and that did scare me. I knew I couldn't believe anything he said.

I asked him point blank how he felt about Sarah.

He said, "She is very young, and her parents got wind of something, and she is not allowed to come around me anymore."

Ummmm, I wonder how that happened.

"You still didn't tell me how you feel about her," I said.

He said he was infatuated, and that he could have loved her.

Ms. Diary, that was all I needed to know.

He asked where I was going, and I told him Memphis, which I had already said. Apparently he wasn't listening. He stood up with fists clenched and told me I wasn't taking his children to a city. Period.

"You don't even have a place to stay, and you think you are taking my children away," he said.

I let him talk. He asked if I even understood what's going on here.

"Yes Evan, I understand that divorce is a bad thing," I said. "I know my reputation will be shot. I know you will have to live with the repercussions here, and I'm sorry about that. I'm sorry you couldn't be sad when you thought I was dying. I'm sorry I wrote you that first letter. I'm sorry about a lot of things, but it changes nothing."

Then I let him ramble on.

My turn again. Short and sweet. "Come Friday morning, I will be taking the kids and moving to Memphis, and yes, I do have a place to stay."

June 17, 1951

*D*ear Diary,

Hello, old friend. It's been a while since I've talked to you. You were always there when I needed you, and you always kept my secrets. Thank you.

Life has changed for me, and I just wanted to tell you some good things after filling you with so many bad things over the years. When I left Evan, I took the kids and moved to Memphis. Fred has a little house here and welcomed us all. When my divorce was final, Fred and I got married. He is so good to me and the children. I finally know what love is.

We have a new baby boy. His name is Johnston Fredrick Dawson. He is five months old. It looks like he may have curly hair like Fred.

Ms. Diary, I had to forgive Evan for my own piece of mind, however, I saw him in town last Wednesday, and was so shocked to see who this man was. Remember how he thought he was too good to do woman's work, like dishes or changing the baby's diaper, bringing wood in for the fire, or milking the cows. Well, it seems he married little Miss Sarah who is ten years his junior. It apparently is not the bed of roses he had anticipated.

I sat down and talked with him a bit. Surprisingly, he was very talkative. It seems Sarah leads him around by the nose, and if he doesn't do what she wants she tells Mommy and Daddy, and they let Evan know who is boss. He works at the bank again, because according to Sarah's mother, it is a more respectable job than farming. He was never good at that either. He hates the bank, and hates his life, and just found out that Sarah is pregnant, which is why they are in Memphis. Her parents didn't think the doctors in Mason were good enough for their daughter.

He is so miserable. He looks older and more haggard than he did when he came home from the war. They live in a little apartment in Mason over the hardware store, and he hates that, too. Evidently, Sarah rules the roost and keeps a steady supply of insults to hurl at him.

While we were talking, Sarah walked in. She didn't even look my way. I said, "Hello, Sarah."

She ignored me and said to Evan, "I told you to meet me in ten minutes, and here you sit on your ass." The look on Evan's face was very telling.

I said, "Evan, I am so sorry." And I truly was.

I stood up to go, and Evan touched my arm. He said, "I passed up chicken and dumplings for a bologna sandwich." It was strange, but I knew exactly what he meant.

Growing up I remember hearing the old folks saying, you made your bed, you lie in it. Now I know what it means.

Ms. Diary, I am sure I'll return soon, but with happy news.

Goodnight Ms. Diary

www.ingramcontent.com/pod-product-compliance
Lightning Source LLC
Chambersburg PA
CBHW050729180626
46814CB00002B/675